THE QUEST

A SANTIAGO PILGRIM STORY

DOUG McPHILLIPS

Also, by Doug McPhillips:

From Darkness to Light.
Awakened to my Gutted Dream.
The Sword of Discernment.
Santiago Traveller.
I, Prophet.
Master's at my table.
The Guru of Jerusalem.
We are upside down. (Biography)
The Wicklow Way.
The Adventures of Ace McDice.
Instant Karma & Grace.
The Credo.
Reflections of an Old Man.
Reincarnation of the Assassin
Masters of Introspection.
Journey to a hermit's haven.
The Rise and Rise of a 4th Reich
Grandad's tales are tall and true.
Into Action: Alcoholics for Jesus
A Pilgrim's Last Hurrah.
Lightbulb Moments
For Pete's sake
Walking in My Shadow
Sweet Surrender
The Camino Diaries

Doug McPhillips, Circa 2026, ISBN 978-1-7643804-4-7
National Library of Australia Catalogue-in-Publication data:
New Holy Bible, International Version, Hodder & Stoughton,
1980. Alcoholics Anonymous, 4th Edition, AA World Service,
1976.

As Bill sees it, 8th Print, AA World Service. 2017
Daily Reflections, 11th Print, AA World Service 2014.
Journey to the Inner Mountain, Hodder & Staughton, 2002.
The Choice is always ours, Jove Publishing, 1997.
The Mythical Journey Simon & Schuster, 1999
The Sword of Discernment, Ingram Spark. Doug McPhillips
2014
Santiago traveller, Ingram Spark, Doug McPhillips, 2018.
Lightbulb Moments, Ingram Spark, Doug McPhillips, 2025.
Sweet Surrender, Imgran Spark, Doug McPhillips, 2026.
The Camino Diaries, Ingram Spark, Doug McPhillips, 2026

For all pilgrims of The Way,
longing for the calling to reflect
on the journey towards the light.

The Preface.

The intent of this book is not like the previous books I have written on the Camino, nor on spiritual matters, nor on my pilgrimage goals and outcomes, resulting in writings of the reality of the journey, the myth, the legend, and the novella of stories within the main storylines, and just as important to me, the many poems and songs that resulted as a consequence. Rather, this book is as much about what I had missed as about what I had experienced, imagined, or achieved. The shape of things to come within is indeed drawn from my three Camino de Santiago as much as other wanderings. Still, it is the awareness I have now in my dottage that captures my attention and, hopefully, yours, dear reader, is written as much in the words as the space in between.

The book may well be a guiding light to a film of the idea in the long run, but in truth, the prospect of filming in a faraway land, whilst appealing to the senses, may well be a pipe dream that is not fulfilled in my lifetime. On reading my Camino books, some enlightened soul in the future may cotton on to the idea for generating that outcome.

I am writing to inform you of what I did not see and do now see, of what was, is, and may well be in the future. So, before delving into the content of this book, we may well refer back to the interview I had with a journalist which has in its entirety the intention of this older man whose days may be numbered, but whose heart still longs for the faraway mountains of the Pyrenees, the hills, valleys and hamlets along The Way, the plains of the Masada, the cities of Burgos, Leon and Santiago, and indeed the end of the earth at Finisterre.

The Interviewer asked, "Why did you walk the Camino?"

Pilgrim: " I wasn't looking for adventure, I was looking for a way to keep moving when standing still seemed impossible."

The Interviewer: " You must have had a good reason?"

Pilgrim: "Every step became a story. From grief, to endurance, to awakening, my books and songs were born on The Way… I walked when things had come apart."

Interviewer: You've walked the Camino three times. Was each walk different from the other?"

Pilgrim: "The first camino was survival, the second was intention, the third was like walking with an old friend. "

Interviewer: " What do you hope people will take away from these insights of the Camino pilgrimages.

Pilgrim: "An awakening of the spirit within."

Content:

Introduction.

The story herein is of my returning to the **Camino de Santiago** for a fourth time. It is not about repeating what has already been discovered; it is about something deeper: less about discovery and more about incorporating the ordinariness of what I have experienced on past pilgrimages into deeper meaning for others and, in turn, being, for me, a quiet transformation. Whilst past Caminos allowed me to reflect on past suffering, lessons on letting go, and a better understanding of the meaning of life, expressed through many books and songs inspired by my journeys for my wellbeing and the benefit of others, they are nonetheless creative expressions of the man that was.

The past Caminos were full of intent to find answers, to express grief, to heal, to gain insight, and to accept. The first Camino was one of curiosity on a road less travelled, of letting go with many creative ideas; the second was an attempt to express love, which led me to understand the mysteries of the soul. The third Camino was one for me, which led to even more writing of inner transformation.

The Camino was always for me a road less travelled that I walked upon. Now, whilst the route to Santiago along The Way hasn't changed for over a thousand years, this pilgrim feels a sense of belonging now. The Camino has become part of me. It calls, and I respond. Not as I once did after writing books, poems and songs about the Camino, but more as an offering to you the reader, as a living continuation of my creative expression embodied in the message from my heart and soul self, a somewhat deeper sharing of wisdom learnt for you in your own suffering, in moments of anxiety and in loss of a loved one or indeed loss of self purpose. This book is more about the ministry of presence, not just in the story. It will, from time to time, give you a sense of the importance of being conscious in the moment, which sometimes is only learned upon reflection.

The destination of the Camino, the focus towards the Santiago de Compostela Cathedral, whilst still having deep religious, spiritual and cultural significance, becomes secondary to the walking itself. For it is in the daily act of walking that inner stillness emerges; it is in the breaking away from the everyday that the meaning of simplicity of living is renewed; and it is in such a state that a confirmation of faith becomes real.

We shall travel over th raw but collective experiences along The Way, over hill; and down dale, through village hamlets, city streets and monuments of the past, churches, temples and cathedrals, steeples, and sunrises over the Meseta; being in communion sharing bread and wine with other pilgrims, and all the while the knowing of the quiet rhythm of walking all day. It comes as a pilgrimage of life because this life on earth keeps unfolding. This fourth Camino symbolises closure of what I have done creatively, it brings to me a touch of gratitude to all those who have given back to me in their own way along The Way, and what may well emerge is a new chapter as the Camino calls me back to something unfinished in my heart, where The Way wishes me to walk again.
The Camino calls again.

On my first Camino de Santiago in 2013, I arrived at St. Jean Pied de Port during the **Fête de la Saint-Jean** (St. John's

Festival), whilst it was in full swing. It is a major, traditional celebration held in May. Still, that year it was the 100th anniversary, so the parade and ceremony went on into the night, with a fleet of floats and period costumes, traditional bonfires, music, and community gatherings.

At the time, I was nursing a headache after a serious fall in Paris the day before and was intent on distracting myself, so the parade was a godsend, as was the food before turning in for the night.

My second Camino was a flight to Paris, then walking the Portuguese Way to Santiago. My mind was more concerned with meeting up with a lady from Lisbon who had volunteered to walk with me. This pilgrimage had me more involved with the distraction of her than the actual journey itself. I had also determined a goal that was indeed another distraction away from the journey of my soul. On my third Camino, I returned to St. Jean again to walk the Way, this time for me as a soul purpose without expectations. Now, despite writing a plethora of books and songs about my pilgrimages, I have had an after-day awakening that I was only half-conscious at the time and missed so much on my way.

Now it is apparent to me that I have awakened from a dream and recall events and situations that I was not formally aware of, but somehow were implanted in my subconscious mind that I now recall like sitting in a cafe on the main cobblestone street of St. Jean early on a summer evening, and being conscious of the quietness of the street compared to my stay there 5 years earlier. I was mindful of the layout of nearby restaurants and the ancient walls enclosing the street opposite.

This time, I had settled into an attic albergue in midtown, where, on my first camino, I had been in another attic much higher up, on the rooftop of a private hotel. It was mid-evening, and soon I headed for bed. Whereas I was on my first Camino, the evening sun had just fallen below the horizon, and I recall the beauty of the sunset behind the silhouette of the Pyrenees mountains. It is clearer to me now, and the memory haunts me like a magnetic draw card, returning me to that exact location and reliving it with renewed desire and consciousness of the nature of it all.

The first flutter of my eyelids upon awakening comes to me now like a vision of the morning light, the sun shining in on my room, begging me to awaken and get on my way. Well before I shouldered my backpack, the view of the empty streets greeted me; the contrast between dark and light shaped the buildings, and doorways and windows reflected the sunlight.

The lone pilgrim sees himself as though he is another; he stands on the bridge at Saint-Jean-Pied-de-Port, gazing down at the stream flowing quietly between its banks, lined with hotels and ancient buildings stretching into the distance. He turns and glances back along the silent, empty street behind him. For a moment, he lingers there, as if acknowledging the world he is about to leave behind. Then, with quiet determination, he lifts the hood of his black parka, tightens the straps of his pack, and picks up his walking poles. Ahead lies the ancient gate of the town. Beyond it, the steep climb into the Pyrenees.

Step by step, he walks through the gate and begins the ascent.

As the mountains rise before him, the sound of his own voice breaks the silence… *"Every journey begins with a single step. But the Camino is more than a road across Spain. It is a road into ourselves. A journey through struggle, memory, loss… and sometimes, healing."*

And so the long road begins.
I was thinking of how, for more than a thousand years, pilgrims have taken this journey of the soul. As I climbed, my mind heard the words of the song I had written, which denotes the meaning of The Quest:

"It's not just a walk in the woods. The Camino Way, the Napoleon route, begins in the foothills of the Pyrenees at St. Jean Pied de Port and ends 800 kilometres away in Santiago, Spain. Across hills and dales, from rugged mountains to valley floors, desert plains, through ancient villages and historic cobblestone streets. It's not for the faint-hearted, this daily grind of one's Camino. Bone weariness, injury or illness, and a feeling of being alone with your thoughts and emotions are constant companions. Fellow pilgrims light the way, and strangers forge bonds of friendship, greeting each other with "Buen Camino," meaning "good journey." The long journey of The Way is not just an outward journey but an inward one. It's a daily reminder that one needs very little of the material world to be happy. Pilgrims have walked The Way for over a thousand years, following the way of St. James, the Apostle of Christ. Some believe his bones are buried under the altar of the Cathedral at Santiago, where the traditional way finishes wth a Christian celebration. Whatever the reasons for one's Camino, it's a long walk, moving from place to place in body, mind, and spirit. A chance to be apart, to breathe in a holy work, to encounter, to glimpse the mystery."

My reflection as I rewalked the Pyrenees track brought back many visions of the sheer beauty of the mountains, the mist over the valley floor below, and the distant ring of the church bells in the village of St. Jean, being drowned out by the sound of cattle bells as they roam the Pyrenees' hilltops.

The memory of stopping at the little hamlet of **Orisson** for coffee seated outside the small albergue overlooking the valley floor below, near the highest point of the Pyrenees route. I am reminded of my diary recording of the day's journey and the pilgrims' greetings as I climbed, as well as the friendly greetings from the local barge people on the route. I had journeyed this route twice before, and nothing had changed except my deeper awareness of the presence of nature and the divine presence in the hearts of those I exchanged greetings with on their Camino, and of the reasons for their individual journeys. I moved on alone, conscious of others' presence but now more intent on my own soul journey. It was like walking across a postcard of nature on a fine ridge above the world. I was high up in the midst of clouds, but in reality, I was grounded to The Way forward.

There was still more mountainous climbing to be done for the next ten kilometres before the descent into the valley floor for the end of the first day's rest at **Roncesvalles,** a further 5 kilometres downward slope to the valley floor below.

My mind also drifted back to my state of mind on previous times I had walked the Pyrenees' mountain ranges and the forests that surrounded the path I trod. Once more, a song came to my mind which I had written in my melancholy state back then. It was befitting that it should return to mind as I travelled the old region where its inspiration had come to me:

I wandered inside myself long before I wandered across Spain or Portugal. I had walked through emotional deserts, through nights where the soul is stretched thin, and the silence becomes a kind of crucifixion. Nights when no one understands your pain. Days when the world feels alien and God unbearably distant. I had been thinking of Cardinal Newmans' cry to God 'Lead kindly light, lead thou me on,' and a song came to me then, not like the Newman hymn itself, but the song I wrote carrying that same essence: the cry of a soul no longer asking for answers, no longer demanding reasons, only begging for a single step of clarity in a darkness too thick to navigate.

In that state, I felt kinship with Christ—not in any grand or theological sense, but in the quiet human truth of suffering that refines, suffering that strips away illusions, suffering that leaves you naked before God with only one prayer left:
"Lead me. Just lead me. I cannot lead myself."
For I, too, had reached a point where the future was obscured, the past uninhabitable, the present unbearable. Like Jesus, I felt abandoned by the structures that once held me. Like Him, I felt the sting of betrayal—by life, by others, by my own expectations. Like Him, I wandered without a resting place, searching for a light I could no longer generate from within.
And in that spiritual homelessness, the Camino became the rough wooden plank I carried across the landscape of my life —a pilgrimage not of choice but of necessity, a way of staggering onward when everything inside wanted to collapse.

This likeness to Christ was never about imitation.

It was recognition. Recognition that loneliness is sacred ground. However, my cry was for the women, not Christ within, then, but in that second Camino, it was the women I saw as a vain substitute. It wasn't until the third camino that this Christ-likeness—not in glory but in desolation—that formed the bridge into my Third Camino. For before surrender comes stripping. Before awakening comes abandonment.

Before resurrection comes the long, cold night of the tomb.

My song "Lead Kindly Light" was not merely created.

It was *birthed*—from loss, from exile, from the feeling of being cast out into darkness with nothing left but a whisper of trust. And that whisper became the compass. The Camino would soon show me that these states of wandering, of passion misplaced, of seeking home in another's arms, of resisting the inner alchemy—were all preparations. Preparations for the surrender are underway.

Lead kindly light
lead thou me on,
keep thou my feet,
upon the path I'm on.

Let me not falter,
to climb the highest hill,
view peaceful valleys,
We're ill at last, be still.

Let me not falter,
To climb the highest hill,
View peaceful valleys,
Where I'll at last be still.

Oh, where are you now
My sweet foreign maid
Blind is the light
Har burns in my brain,

Foxes have holes,
Birds have their nest,
But this weary pilgrim
Has no place to rest.

Oh! where are you now,
My sweet foreign maid
Hid by the light
That burns in my brain?

The climb to Leoeder, on the way to **Roncesvalles**, was a total of seventeen kilometres and almost 1,500 metres up. It was then a slow walk down the steep incline to the valley floor, a shortcut I remembered among the heavy wooden trees that served as props to slow the pace when my legs began to falter. It was then, ten kilometres later, that I arrived at the cosy medieval hamlet of Roncesvalles. As always at the end of a day's hiking, I looked forward to a shower, a hot meal, and the pleasure of fresh bread and a non-alcoholic beer, as was my custom. I then visited the medieval **Iglesia de Santa Maria.**

The Concventus Hospitalis Roncesvalles was my first albergue on the Camino. At this rest stop, hundreds of pilgrims seek refuge after a long 26-kilometre walk over the Pyrenees mountains and down to the valley floor, marking the end of day 1 on the Camino. It was my custom to visit the abbey archives to revisit the story of Roland, the 11th-century hero of battle and song.

As previously, I had bypassed the lower route past the monument to **Roland** at Alto de Barieta. Roland was the nephew of Charlemagne, the famous general and, ultimately, king of France in the 11th century. Roland died in 778 defending the rear guard of Charlemagne's army against the Moors on their return via the lower Pyrenees route to France after defeating the Muslims in many battles throughout the Spanish kingdom.

Tramping of The Way.

The battle between Roland and the Moorish giant, fought to the death, reached mystical proportions, inspired the epic poem "Roland's Song," the first recorded poem in French history, and served as a catalyst for the creation of the myth of Camelot and King Arthur. The Knights of the Round Table, the singing sword of Arthur, embedded in the rock, has similarities with Roland's sword, buried in a rock near where the monument stands today, but ten kilometres from Roncesvalles Pass.

 I had been remembering my stories: "The Master of the Arts" and "Merlin and the Singing Swords," which I had written somewhat motivated by my Camino journeys and visits to the Pyrenees region.

It was where, on both my previous stays, I found myself sleeping in a bunk bed in the bowels of the old abbey's sleeping quarters, between the building's foundation pillars—a fitting location for a pilgrim's own soul foundations to contemplate.

I blew out the candle, and the shadows of night crept into my dreamtime. However, I couldn't take the recall of the dreams of knights in battle, of Roland's sword embedded in a rock, of King Arthur extricating the singing sword from a rock to become king of Camelot, and the rough sound of people on the move. The flashing of the headlamps in my eyes and the things that go bump in the night disturbed my slumber. It would be commonplace on my Camino pilgrimages. It was no less the case in Roncesvalles. Something I took for granted in my travels, as I had always done, even in the boarding school years of my youth. Those sounds and whispers of other pilgrims on the move in total darkness, keen to get an early start on their Camino, had me always on the move early, too. Here I was on hallowed ground, tramping where Charlmange and his army had marched in the 11th century, and where thousands of pilgrims had walked before me. I recalled these grounds had once been blood-soaked from battle, since the tears of pilgrims who had passed over. The spirit of the dead seemed to hang before me as the morning sun rose above the horizon.

I was soon on the main pathway of The Way, and the scallop-shell markers appeared every few kilometres as constant reminders, as did the yellow arrow signs of the Camino.

Near the road junction, the first eatery appeared, offering a place to eat. Whilst it was better than walking on an empty stomach, the food was not very nourishing, as it sold mainly groceries, cake, and flavoured milk. There was a notice board above the door with a sign that said Ernest Hemingway had stopped to eat at the same spot on his way to Pamplona for the Running of the Bulls celebration. I thought of his passion for bullfights and recalled the description of a bullfight in his book, "Death in the Afternoon." I had wondered if Hemingway ever passed on the Camino Way. To my knowledge, he had never written about The Camino in any of his many novels with a Spanish flavour. Still, as a marketing man myself, I thought it enterprising of the shop owner to advertise that Hemingway had called therein. In consideration of the discomfort from the food I had consumed, I began walking along the long river flats in the shade of forest trails, past rivers and small villages, and towards **Zubiri**, my destination for that day.

I recalled an intriguing story I had read about King Gougia in the magnum opus of ancient Chinese literature of the 5th century. Apparently, the King was captured by his arch-enemy and imprisoned for three years before being granted amnesty. Rather than return to his throne, he resolved to eat peasant food and live simply. He slept on a bed of rough wood. He licked a gall bladder every day as a reminder that tasting life's bitterness embedded the constant shame and humiliation he had suffered in captivity, and this he drew strength from. The memory of that story bolstered my spirit, for I had then resolved to live on that malnourished so-called breakfast for the remainder of the day. I did wonder, in hindsight, how I managed to maintain my energy to make my way to **Zuriri** in the sweltering heat that day.

Suppose Hemingway had eaten at that little supply ship, what might he have eaten to get him all the way to Pamplona? In 2017, I got up late in an albergue in Roncesvalles, ate a hearty breakfast, and tramped on with a group of young pilgrims in the spirit of delight, feeling the pilgrim company and the freedom of youth embrace me.

It had proved to be a beautiful day for walking, and in the company of fellow pilgrims. The pathway at some 1000 metres above sea level was easy going for the majority of the 23.3 km to **Zubiri**, lightened by the spirit of those who walked with me. The forest walkways and the oasis of charming little villages ease the burden of my heavy backpack in the blistering heat.

Recalling my first Camino pilgrimage and the physical suffering I endured from an overloaded backpack, blistered feet, and heat exhaustion, and the fact that I found no accommodation in Zubiri, my zeal and resolve were tested to the full on that second day. The second time around, I had better luck in one sense: the mid-summer heat turned to wet weather, but that too had its discomforts. As I think about it now, I recall that in such moments of great physical effort and pain, the creative juices would flow, and often melodies and lyrics for a song would spring forth from my imagination. It was in such a moment of recall that my "Walking the Camino" song came to mind. It was on my second Camino on the French route that I sang it to the young people I was walking with. The catchiness of that tune has since earned it record airplay in Canada, the USA and Germany. Tunecore reported that it was the most-played song of 2025. And now, after all these years of creating, there comes a quiet willingness to let go. To loosen my hold on all that the world says should matter.

I no longer seek to be understood. Nor do I walk with the same anticipation as before. Instead, I am drawn toward a deeper awareness—one that sits beyond the need for expression, even after all the words I have written.

And still, I find myself seeking.

It now seems inconsequential that many of my stories and songs came to me on The Camino, but it has me reflecting more on the spiritual aspects of what is going on here than on the creative output that has resulted.

On my first Camino, I had struggled on alone, without companionship, unable to find accommodation, and travelling past Zubiri and on to **Akerreta**, arriving at an albergue by the river early evening and finding only a soup kitchen opened to feed my hunger. The remaining 21km to Pamplona the next day was easier, as I had treated blistered feet and surgically removed a toenail in a somewhat primitive act of modus operandi.

My entry into **Pamplona** on the first pilgrimage was at a time of heightened celebration for the feast of St. Fermin, the Spanish bishop who died as a martyr for his faith but was dragged by his enemies through the streets by bulls to his death. I had caught up with a Viking-like redheaded Irishman, a middle-aged pilgrim and a man of pleasant company and historic fact, as he was a lecturer in history back in Dublin. It was a memorable occasion for me as I recall our stroll over the remaining few kilometres into the city. Willie, as I recall, had prebooked his accommodation and suggested I might check out his hotel, as the city he advised would be pretty much booked out due to the festival.

I recall the sense of subdued excitement entering a bustling, crowded central plaza full of happy-go-lucky people dressed in period costumes, others, particularly young Spanish men, in the traditional garb of white shirts, black pants over Spanish leather boots and a red sash around the waist or tucked in anticipation of a pending fight with a bull. The running of the bulls was over now; it was time for dancing in the street, eating at outdoor restaurants and cafes, and drinking copious quantities of wine in the merriment of the moment.

I followed Willie like a lost sheep to his hotel, and with typical Irish charm, he convinced the innkeeper to grant me accommodation at a moderate fee. We had agreed to meet in the foyer an hour later to catch up with a friend of his for a meal. However, this did not eventuate, for as soon as I made it to the room, i lay on the bed and fell into a deep sleep for another hour and a half. By the time I showered and entered the foyer, Willie had long gone. I never did see that Irishman again in my travels.

My meandering through the streets of Pamplona in search of a restaurant led me to a bar for tapas and drinks. There, I met up with a couple of Irish women, a mother and daughter I had met on my first day in the Pyrenees Mountains. We ate, and they drank. I contented myself with zero alcohol beer and Tapas, whilst their intake of white wine was never-ending. I lost count after their twelfth wine, and constant calls to the barman for "one more, no more" echoed in my head. We left the bar together and meandered back to the Plaza del Castillo central square, where I wished them farewell and followed the winding, narrow lane back to my hotel.

My return to Pamplona some five years later was not as memorable. Still, I do recall entering the city with a group of youth singing my "Walking the Camino ' song with a strong chorus from my fellow companions of the Way at the time. Some flashbacks of visits to the Cathedral, a statue of bulls and the saint behind a picketed iron fence, and Hemingway's lair where he wrote 'Death in the Afternoon.' A timely recall of this fair city's three days of celebration of the running of the bulls. Then, on my exit from the city after the festivities, I entered villages, continuing to celebrate the fight with bulls and almost got caught up in the scramble for a local bull run through the streets. The latter journey was also a timely reminder when a high-speed train travelling to a major Catholic pilgrimage destination in Spain derailed at over 190 km/h in an 80 km/h zone, killing some 80 people and injuring over 100. Driver Francisco José Garzón Amo was charged with reckless homicide after a distracted moment, with safety failings also cited. I heard the news of this while I had a brief coffee break as I exited the city limits.

It is not always happy thoughts that the mind retains as memorable; it serves as a further reminder that, when it comes to death, we do not know the time nor the hour. It serves to always be on guard against being drawn into the shadow self rather than the revelations of the light.

My memories of Pamplona now fade into the background as I recall the long ascent to the "hill of Forgiveness," where the pilgrim statue of the 'alto' reminds me of the thousands of pilgrims who have walked this path for centuries. The 360-degree panoramic view of Pamplona and the valley below remains a beautiful memory. The descent to **Puente la Reina** (Queens Bridge) is no less memorable, and the medieval alleys and the impressive 11th-century bridge over the Arga River are still wonders to behold in my memory bank.

The Camino memories I tramped through to **Estella** and the free wine fountain at the Bodegas Irache museum. I recall I watched as many pilgrims enjoyed alcoholic refreshments, but did not partake. I had sworn myself off alcohol after my former life and blamed in no small way my alcoholic behaviour had been instrumental in the breakdown of my marriage. It was best to leave those thoughts in the shadows of the past. The Way had proved tiring but even now brings pleasant recall of passing vineyards, olive trees and cereal crops across the rolling countryside on the 23.8 km stretch of road to **Puente La Reina**. The hot, dry weather of July 2013 was almost more than one could bear, but in contrast, in 2017, it rained cats and dogs for the whole journey, and I lived constantly in wet clothing. Those days and nights on the road are part of the trial of doing one's penance, letting go of the world to embrace the spiritual aspects of acceptance in whatever came my way. It holds no other particular significance in my memory other than that of my pilgrimage out of the night of the soul into the light of life to live, now and really live!

The first part of my pilgrimage was a time of letting go of all the pain and heartache of losing family and a son by his own hand. It was a time of attempting to heal, with no agenda other than walking. In truth, though, I had not surrendered my worldly desires; I had set a goal to bring back home something symbolic of my pilgrimage. It turned out to be my diary and an idea for a book. It was, in fact, to me, continuing that process of writing copious thoughts and feelings, coupled with my desire to find something unexplainable that still alluded me.

Even after completing the first Camino, I had envisaged a second Camino, with the desire to embrace another woman in my search for inner happiness. I had not, at the realisation that the ' kingdom of heaven ' is within. It was always the women I was drawn to, not the God of my own understanding. The answer to the riddle of love doesn't come through the lust of the heart, as life had surely taught me. Letting go and moving on did ultimately happen to me, as reflected in my writings and songs. Life has its own way of working out whether we have the patience to persevere with whatever is predaily.

There was a certain animal-like awareness of my surroundings as I walked through the heat of the day in 40-degree Celsius temperatures. I recalled I had planned to walk the 23.8 km from Pamplona to Puente la Reina, but the extreme heat had got the better of me. I settled for an albergue not far from **Uterga**, some 18 km from Pamplona, a little short of my planned pilgrimage trudge for the day. The albergue was a medieval hermitage, a quaint abode for a weary traveller. There was little of this world's sights to see, but a hearty meal I had in what was an upmarket restaurant for such an isolated place, in what was surrounded by desert. There was once a basilica and a pilgrims' hospice, but now the main landmark was a nearby hilltop with forty windmills that provided electricity for the region. A sign nearby was inscribed , "Dónde se cruzó el camino del viento con el de las estrellas." Where the way of the wind meets the way of the stars.

After the pleasantries of a hot meal and warm shower, I settled for treating my blistered feet before a final prayer in the hope of a correo (post office) not too far distant down the track, to offload some of my heavy pack and send the excess baggage on to Santiago. It seemed I slept heavily for but a few hours back, but the upside was I was on the move again before dawn, and I recall passing through **Uterga** before daybreak and hearing the sound of church bells ringing in the small village of **Obanos,** off the beaten track.

The sight of the famous six-arch Romanesque Bridge over the Rio Arga at Puente la Reina came into view after my slow trudge through wheat fields and vineyards. It was at a small cafe for breakfast and a coffee before venturing over the bridge.

Although it has been 13 years since I sat in that cafe and ate my breakfast, the memory of that place is embedded in my memory. In my aloneness and many days of isolation until that day, it was the beginning of a new direction in my life, although I had not been aware of it then. For it was here I met two German backpackers, and one of whom would be a catalyst to my writing songs and books over the years that have followed to this very day.

The universe works in strange ways, and it is often after much mental or physical suffering—such as the pain of loss, loneliness, a physical accident, or a loss of direction in life, among many other tragic circumstances—that these hardships come to the surface, forcing us to look deep within. It is then that creativity comes to the rescue, flowing from our inner child or the spirit world of our muse. In those moments, we are freed from the burden that has led us to sadness, reaching a high point of expression from our hearts in positive output for our own healing and for the benefit of others.

In crossing the famous Romanesque bridge at Puente la Reina in the company of the young German rock musician and his good companion, I was led into the joys of youthful pranks and stories of old that gladdened my old heart. I never would have guessed at the time that a simple poem written under great duress would lead to a song. Then, a burst of creative output that astounded me as much as it had friends and family followed on my return home from that first Camino adventure.

When I sit and contemplate it all, I, too, am astounded. I shall tell more about this as I recall in sequence to the journey that follows herein. The creative output was profound enough, but what followed had to grow into a sense of international connectedness until after my third Camino. The song that has been consistently played on the radio across the northern hemisphere was one I wrote on my return home after the first journey of The Way. Many times, I have sung this song along with pilgrims on the Caminos that followed. It summed up my life at the time and is worth repeating here, but it's not how I see things today.

I'm walking the Camino,
on the way to Santiago,
Yeah, I'm leaving here today,
'cause I'm on my way,
walking the Camino,

I'm walking the Camino,
on the way to Santiago,
got my knapsack on my back,
heading down the track,
walking the Camino,
walking the Camino.

Oh! I used to call you honey,
till you spent all my money,
No use looking back,
just heading down the track,
walking the Camino,
walking the Camino.

Well, I had a life of plenty,
until the pile was empty,
wine, women and song,
The pleasures are all gone,
So, I'm walking the Camino,
walking the Camino.

I'm walking the Camino,
on the way to Santiago,
Yeah, I'm leaving here today,
cause I am on my way,
walking the Camino,

Walking the Camino.
singing me this song,
walking the Camino,
walking the Camino.

Walking in God's space.

The walk from **Estella to Los Argos** with my new band of young brothers left me deep in thought. Even then, I was looking for answers as I wandered through the lovely Monjardin village and along the long, flat track—and continual tramping over rolling hills, with no relief from the relentless sun beating down. Where no one dared to stay, we wandered like lost sheep searching for our own way home, with the goal of Santiago always in our minds, even though we hadn't experienced the inner life. They were, nonetheless, on their rite of passage, while all I sought was to let go of a life I knew without much awareness of what lay ahead.

There has always been something in my Camino—and in the many journeys beyond it—that has drawn me outside the confines of the logical, linear world. Out there, I found a kind of freedom that I could never fully grasp within the structures of ordinary life.

I came to these paths through suffering—through despair, loneliness, and a deep unravelling of the self. Yet from that breaking emerged a wellspring of creativity: words, songs, stories shaped from both reality and imagination, from myth and memory. For a time, it felt as though I had found something—and perhaps even understood it.

But the journey does not end there. What was once gained now feels as though it is being gently reversed, or perhaps stripped back. The shadow returns—not as something to fear, but as something still to be understood. And now, after all these years of creating, there comes a quiet willingness to let go. To loosen my hold on all that the world says should matter.

I no longer seek to be understood. Nor do I walk with the same anticipation as before. Instead, I am drawn toward a deeper awareness—one that sits beyond the need for expression, even after all the words I have written.

And still, I find myself seeking.

There is a consciousness I have not yet reached—something that gives greater meaning to the simple act of walking the Way. The Camino, and the many paths that echo it, are no longer just journeys across land, but movements within the soul—following the traces of those who came before, each walking their own quiet pilgrimage.

Now, the awakenings come differently.

They rise not from the striving of the moment, but from memory—from the small, unnoticed things along the way that I once passed by without understanding. And it is here, in these fragments, that something new begins to form.
The question now is not how to explain it, but how to live it— and perhaps, in time, how to share it in a way that might gently guide those who follow. And in doing so, to hear it more clearly within myself... as I continue to walk, still seeking the deeper purpose that binds meaning to this life.

Perhaps it lies in the longing for another—the "other" that always seems just beyond reach. Or perhaps the answer is not an answer at all, but a question that was never meant to be resolved. Maybe it is found in nature—in the quiet voice that whispers of love without asking anything in return. Whatever it may be, I have longed for it then, just as I do now. I once believed it lived in the love of a woman—the warmth, the closeness, the fleeting sense of being whole. And yet, deep down, I have always known it is not the woman herself I seek. It is something deeper. It is the presence of God within the heart and soul of man. And still, there remains a sadness—a quiet, lingering loneliness. The touch of a woman, the holding of another, can ease it for a moment—but only for a moment.

When she moves on, as they so often do, the emptiness returns. A man is left exposed, stripped back to himself, carrying both memory and silence. There is beauty in those memories—but the wisdom of pain shapes them.

And so I find myself reflecting more deeply now than before. What once felt like loss begins to reveal something else— something I could not see at the time. I pray, as I always have, for love to come—not simply to fill the emptiness, but to transform it. To take this quiet sadness and turn it into understanding… or perhaps into peace. For this feeling is not new. I wrote of it then. And it remains with me still.

And so I walk on in the memory of it all —no longer searching for something to find, but perhaps to become. Still listening and still learning. Still seeking that deeper purpose that binds meaning to this life… one step at a time along the Way.

The path from **Los Argos** passed through endless fields that would have been ready for harvest, but on that first Camino, it had not rained for months, and the land was just a desert plain. My young band of brothers had stayed behind in some village on The Way. I drifted on tramping, now remembering the Belgian beauty who, around dusk, ventured off the beaten path to seek refuge at a deserted old hamlet at **San Bol,** where St. Anthony had established another hospital in his mission across northern Spain to treat a skin condition known as "St. Anthony's fire."

It was a rather primitive treatment: immersing the patient in cold water during the winter season. It was considered, then, a miracle of sorts, but perhaps the shock to the body was what resulted in the cure. The cure was worse than the disease. It must have worked through, for the record, that St. Anthony set up some sixteen hospitals along the route to Santiago during those medieval times to cure pilgrims. It was in itself a miracle. Some Christians would have it that the Saint's prayers for each of his patients were instrumental in the cure.

And now it comes to me again -there has always been something in my Camino—and in the many journeys beyond it—that has drawn me outside the confines of the logical, linear world. Out there, I found a kind of freedom that I could never fully grasp within the structures of ordinary life.

I came to these paths through suffering—through despair, loneliness, and a deep unravelling of the self. Yet from that breaking emerged a wellspring of creativity: words, songs, and stories shaped from both reality and imagination, from myth and memory. For a time, it felt as though I had found something—perhaps even understood it, but the journey does not end there.

What I was recalling was once gained, now feels as though it is being gently stripped away. The shadow returns—not as something to fear, but as something still to be understood. And now, after all these years of creating, there comes a quiet willingness to let go. To loosen my hold on all that the world says should matter.

I no longer seek to be understood. Nor do I walk with the same anticipation as before. Instead, I am drawn toward a deeper awareness—one that sits beyond the need for expression, even after all the words I have written. And still, I find myself seeking to understand.

The next part of the journey took me across lands that, in the wet season, would have been alive with vineyards and fields of golden wheat. But on that day, the earth was parched, dry, cracked, and silent beneath my feet. As I climbed toward the hilltop towns of **Los Arcos** and on to **Torres del Río**, the weight of the land seemed to mirror something within me. Passing through a small village, I noticed birds circling in the still air, searching the ground for what little sustenance remained. There was no breeze, no movement—only a quiet persistence in their flight.

It was the season when the land should have been full, generous with life. Yet nature, in that moment, seemed more in tune with my inner state than with its own rhythm.

I remember as I entered **La Rioja,** a region known for its richness—for its vineyards and its deep red wines—I found no desire for such things. The promise of abundance meant little to me then. I walked on toward **Logroño**, not in search of pleasure, but simply because the Way continued forward.

Nature, God, and man—these felt distant to me. I was emptied of them, or perhaps unable to feel them. I moved through what felt like the slings and arrows of an unseen force, my body struggling under the heat and the weight of my pack. Each step was an effort. Each breath carried the dryness of the land into me. I was parched—physically and inwardly.

And yet, I continued.

There was a kind of mental anguish that walked beside me, an unrelenting presence that pressed in from all sides. I was alone in every visible sense. And still, somewhere deep within, there was a quiet voice that told me I was not.

That knowing stayed with me, even as I could not fully grasp it. And so I walk on—through dry earth and memory alike—no longer searching for something to find, but perhaps to become. Still listening and still learning. Still seeking that deeper purpose that binds meaning to this life… one step at a time along the Way.

Perhaps it lies in the longing for another—the "other" that always seems just beyond reach. Or perhaps the answer is not an answer at all, but a question never meant to be resolved. Maybe it is found in nature—in the quiet voice that whispers of love without asking anything in return.

My mind drifted to the last time I had that walk, The Way again. As it was for me, the Camino is never the same road twice. On my last journey along this route, the land was not at all dry. It rained without mercy—day after day, night after night. I walked through it, carrying a heavy dose of influenza, my body weakened, my spirit tested in different ways.
I would go to bed wearing the driest clothes I had left, wrapped in what little warmth I could preserve. And in the morning, I would rise only to crawl back into wet clothing, pull on soaked socks, and force my feet into waterlogged boots. Then I would step out again into the rain and begin the slow, relentless trudge forward.

I remember the loneliness of the road from **Logroño** to **Nájera**. The rain blurred the edges of the world, reducing everything to movement and endurance. There was no beauty in it then—only persistence.

Somewhere along that stretch, near the ruins of **San Antón Monastery,** I found refuge in a small café. I sat there, cradling a hot coffee in my hands, trying to bring life back into my fingers. I did my best to dry what I could—socks, layers, fragments of comfort—while the rain continued its quiet assault outside.

It was there that I opened my diary and began to write the notes I had missed earlier in the day, when the rain had made even that simple act impossible.

And then—unexpectedly—she appeared—a Belgian woman, arriving like something out of another world. For a moment, she broke through the isolation, stepping into my space with a warmth that felt almost unreal. There was a closeness, an embrace—human, immediate, undeniable. As I held her, she whispered, "Oh my God."And in that fleeting instant, something shifted. It did not last. These moments rarely do. But it was enough. Enough to remind me of connection. Enough to awaken something that had been buried beneath the cold and the rain. It became, as so many moments on the Camino do, a catalyst—a seed for another song, another expression of something I was still trying to understand. Perhaps it lies in the longing for another—the "other" that always seems just beyond reach. Or perhaps the answer is not an answer at all, but a question never meant to be resolved. Maybe it is found in nature—in the quiet voice that whispers of love without asking anything in return. Or in these brief encounters—these passing reflections of something deeper. Whatever it may be, I have longed for it then, just as I do now. I once believed it lived in the love of a woman—the warmth, the closeness, the fleeting sense of being whole. And yet, deep down, I have always known it is not the woman herself I seek. It is something deeper. It is the presence of God within the heart and soul of man. And still, there remains a sadness—a quiet, lingering loneliness. The touch of another can ease it for a moment—but only for a moment. And when it passes, a man is left again with himself, carrying memory, longing, and the quiet wisdom that pain leaves behind. And so I walk on—through dry earth and relentless rain like—no longer searching for something to find, but perhaps to become. Still listening and still learning. Still seeking that deeper purpose that binds meaning to this life…one step at a time along the Way.

I met the Goddess of beauty.
From Logroño to Nájera
Like a magic link to heaven
As we walked arm in arm.
She held me oh so closely.

It was just a moment in time
I kissed her gently on the cheek
Our spirits were entwined.

"Oh my God," she cried out
"Oh my God, " cried he,
" Oh my God, Oh my God"
" Oh my God", cried we.

So I walked the beat of Mesada
To the ruins of St. Anton
There was music playing in a nearby cafe
So I just drifted on in.

My soul was drawn to the music
A haunting Celtic sound
It took me to my inner self
So I wrote my journal down.

It was there I heard her calling
A Goddess for all to see
She was there in that place, standing
They're right next to me.

I took her in my arms.
She embraced me lovingly
I felt the beating of her heart
Then an angel appeared to me.

We left the cafe together.
Alone with just our thoughts
The beauty of an angel
And the gift of a loving heart.

When we reached the Nagera River,
It was a long farewell.
She said she would see me again sometimes:
Now, how was I to tell?

I lost the Goddess near Carreo
On the Camino Way
She met another heart like mine
She bid me fond farewell.

Now she writes to me from Belgium
As I walk this peaceful day
thinking of our time together
As we walked the Camino Way.

" Oh! My God," she cried out,
" Oh! My God," cried he.
" Oh! My God, Oh! My God,"
" Oh! My God," cried we.

The Reflections of a Soul.

I see it clearly now—I've come further than I realised. The spirit of this worldly man isn't the way it used to be. I'm not inside it anymore—I'm looking at it as it was. What I thought was real wasn't the moment. It was my interpretation of it. She had her own, just as real to her. We were both living inside it. I can see it clearly now—without distortion. And that's more useful to me than holding onto it. I can let it go. I know what comes next…As I write this, my mind drifts back to the long, lonely stretch between **Nájera** and **Santo Domingo de la Calzada**—first in the dry, relentless heat of June 2013, and then again in 2017, when the rain in Spain truly flooded the plain. That initial Camino along that exposed path, stripped of its usual vineyards and fields of grain, starkly contrasted with the second. I was walking not only without a map but also in a different headspace—disconnected, uncertain, guided only by the distances I had jotted down between towns. At one point, I devoured the route entirely and found myself at a literal and internal crossroads, with no clear idea of which way to turn. It was there, during that pause and moment of reckoning, that I looked up and saw, far in the distance, a small group of pilgrims climbing a hill. I set off across the countryside towards them and, in doing so, found my way back onto the Camino. That experience settled something within me. I resolved then that, at the earliest opportunity, I would find a proper guidebook.

When I finally reached **Santo Domingo,** tired but determined, I headed straight to the tourist office for a map. Instead, I stumbled upon a small bookshop where, almost improbably, I found the only English-language guide—*A Hiking Guide to* *the Camino de Santiago*. It felt less like chance and more like an answer. Perhaps, after all, something had been listening.

The hours fade between my first arrival in the square and my return four years later. That initial trip, I carried the weight of losing what I thought defined my worth in the world. I was raw, unsure, and walking simply to let go. By the time I came back, I had gone through encounters that felt like love but turned out to be something lesser—shadows of a deeper truth I still hadn't fully understood. Still wounded, but steadier now, I arrived with a quiet resolve: to move forward, to let go, and to trust in something beyond myself.

On that first Camino, the journey was shaped by fleeting connections with other pilgrims, each walking their own path toward something sacred, or just away from pain. There was an unspoken understanding shared in the rhythm of our steps. I had little to offer in the way of wisdom—no answers, no guidance—only small acts of kindness: a word of encouragement, a pair of scissors to cut a bandage, help for a blistered foot. If anything, I handed over fragments—lines of a song, a broken smile. I knew very little then, but in that emptiness, there was the start of a different kind of knowing.
I had passed through the city's myths—stories that some locals still held as truth. It took a stranger like me to quietly question them, to see the gaps, to recognise where belief and story blurred. Yet it was never my place to challenge them any more than it was theirs to dispute mine. Much of what I had been taught to accept could just as easily be seen as myth. In the same way, I began to understand that I, too, was shaped by stories—constructs formed to give meaning, or perhaps to

My mind, like my body, was walking on foreign soil. It drifted often to the people who had influenced my decision to journey to Santiago, their voices and memories woven into each step. There was an intensity to it—a kind of quiet obsession—where my outward journey became an expression of something unfolding within. Discernment, more than destination, had become my purpose. And so I continued, trampling the Way, not just in search of answers, but in the act of uncovering what was already there. I'd deeper fears, offered up in prayer to an unknown God.

I remember reading from an author—whose name now escapes me—that sometimes lessons aren't fully realised until the teacher has moved on to a different way of living or has passed away. At the time, you sense their presence holds meaning, that they are there for a reason—to guide you, to teach you something, to help you uncover who you are or who you're meant to become. Yet more often than not, you don't truly recognise who they are in your life until much later. They might be a friend, a neighbour, a lover, or even a stranger encountered only briefly along the way.

There is an intuition in those moments—something unspoken that tells you, from the moment your eyes meet, that this person will leave a mark on your life. Sometimes the events that follow feel difficult, even painful or unfair. But with time and reflection, it becomes clear that without those encounters —without facing and moving through those challenges—you may never have discovered your own strength, resilience, or capacity to love. And sometimes, it takes more than one meeting, more than one lesson, before the truth settles in: to embrace what is, to let go of what was, and to keep moving forward.

Such was the case with my encounter with Brother John of the Order of Mother Teresa. Time and again, our paths would cross. He was a tall man, blue-eyed and fair-haired, dressed in a simple white habit, tied at the waist with a Franciscan-style cord. On the front of his garment was an image of Mother Teresa, large and unmistakable, almost the size of an A4 sheet. On his feet were worn black leather sandals, the kind one might expect of a friar. He carried no backpack—only a small shoulder bag—moving lightly along the Way, as though unburdened by more than just possessions.

My own rhythm was different, yet somehow it brought me into his presence again and again. I would rise early, long before most pilgrims stirred, and set out into the day. After a brief stop for coffee and toast, and time to write in my diary, I would continue—sometimes alone, sometimes alongside familiar faces who appeared and disappeared along the journey. At the end of each day, it became my habit to pause at a small chapel if I came upon one. There I would set down my pack, remove my boots, and take in the stillness—studying the architecture, or simply sitting in quiet reflection before moving on to find a place for the night. And more often than not, it was in these sacred spaces that I would find Brother John again, kneeling near the altar, absorbed in prayer.

It remained a quiet mystery to me how he was always ahead of me, despite my early starts and the steady pace I kept each day. I would set out before most pilgrims had even risen, limiting my stops to little more than coffee, a piece of toast, and a few moments to write. Yet somehow, without fail, I would arrive at a chapel or resting place and find Brother John already there, kneeling in prayer, as though he had been waiting all along. It was not until I had walked the earthen paths through the hills of **Montes de Oca** and continued along the forested stretch toward **San Juan de Ortega** that the mystery finally revealed itself.

Two young, devout teachers had invited me to attend Mass in the small chapel adjoining the albergue—an oasis at the edge of the open, barren stretch that followed the forested path. Like the other pilgrims, I took part in the service and received communion. And there, as if placed within the moment itself, was Brother John, once again on his knees in prayer.

When the Mass had ended, I left to join the other pilgrims for a simple meal in a hall frequented by the resident monks. The accommodation had been offered by donation, and the meal was freely given, prepared from their modest supplies. It carried with it a quiet humility, a sense of generosity without expectation. And still, even as I moved on from the chapel into the company of others, Brother John remained behind, kneeling in prayer—unchanged, unmoved, and somehow always ahead.

The night was restless. It took me ages to fall asleep, and when I finally did, I was suddenly woken by the noise of Italian cyclists preparing for an early start. It was only 3:30 a.m., yet they were already on the move. Their voices echoed in the dark, and the flashing of their headlamps cut sharply across my eyes.

…the sudden intrusion shattered what little rest I had managed to find. Pilgrims' voices echoed down the narrow corridor, sharp and urgent, as though the road itself was calling them forward. Then came the metallic clatter of panniers, the whirr of tyres, and the piercing sweep of headlamps cutting through the darkness like restless spirits searching for a path. I lay there, half-awake, half-lost in dreams, caught between irritation and resignation. Sleep, once broken, refused to return easily. Instead, I drifted in that uneasy space where thoughts grow louder, and the body refuses to settle. The room felt smaller, the night longer. And yet, in that moment, there was something else—something strangely familiar about the disturbance. The realisation of constant change was the Camino, after all. It never truly sleeps. There is always someone arriving, someone leaving, someone chasing the dawn for reasons known only to them. Each pilgrim moves to their own rhythm, their own urgency, their own need.

Sleep was no longer an option. I decided to get up and follow suit. In the darkness, I dressed, shouldered my backpack, and headed outside. By the time I reached the courtyard, the cyclists had already gone, their lights fading into the distance. I was standing there in complete darkness. I set down my pack and fumbled for my headlamp. Then, in that moment, a figure appeared—almost ghostlike—draped in a bright white garment. It was Brother John. Without hesitation, he moved forward onto the Way. In that instant, the mystery was solved. He'd always been ahead because he'd started before the rest of us. I quickly lifted my pack, grabbed my walking poles, and followed in his footsteps into the night.

Brother John, whom I came to know later, moved so swiftly along the track and in that semi-darkness, all I could see was a white, ghost-like apparition guiding my way. He moved so quickly and suddenly left the pathway ahead to follow a narrow track. I had no choice but to follow. Soon he stopped at the edge of the track, turned, half-turned away from me, lifted his garment, and turned his head, no doubt aware of my presence, and said: "I'm just taking a piss!"

We returned to The Way. He introduced himself as Brother John, of the brotherhood of Mother Teresa. It wasn't long before I understood his whole spiritual conversion—a university professor by trade—who gave up the life of the first world to become a good Samaritan of the road. He had walked the Camino nine times before his current pilgrimage. And in the tradition of the order, he never carried money, water, or any material goods except for a pair of shorts and a T-shirt. He didn't need to, for he stayed wherever rest was available. Pilgrims came carrying burdens, as I had. Burdens of grief, of guilt, of longing to be free. Some walked for themselves, seeking healing, forgiveness, or peace. Others walked for reasons far beyond their own lives, as Brother John did.

In medieval times, some walked the Camino on behalf of others—souls paid to carry burdens not their own. A pilgrimage undertaken in the name of someone unable, unwilling, or perhaps unworthy to walk it themselves. It was believed that through this act, grace could be transferred, that forgiveness might be granted, that one life could, in some mysterious way, redeem another.

Brother John, of the Order of Mother Teresa, lived streetwise, gained his accommodation by donation, ate the free breakfasts offered by such places, and entered restaurants' kitchens via the back door in the evening, begging his meal from the cook.

More often than not, he was well fed, got water from the fountains in the village square, and did his best to help others on his pilgrimages. John was what you might call 'Camino-wise.' He inquired where I came from, and when I said "Sydney, Australia," he acknowledged by saying, "King's Cross, a bad place." I well knew that from the days of my misspent youth.

The surprising thing was the cleanliness of John's habit; it remained spotless despite the dust and grime of the trail, especially during our time together on the Masada plain. He remarked that kind souls washed it for him, so it stayed pristine and white regardless of the weather or location. It was not long before he, an athletic young man, had left me tramping alone at my own pace. When I caught up with him later in Burgos at an albergue, he handed me a small crucifix with a gentle reminder: "Jesus is guiding you."

Later, I was inspired to write a song with John in mind, as I had seen myself as a beggar along the Way, even outside the Cathedral of Santiago de Compostela, where many stood.

Santiago Traveller.

There's a story that the Christ man told of a pilgrim on his way from Jerusalem to Jericho on that fateful day.

Fortune wasn't smiling when he came across some thieves;
they robbed him, stabbed him,
and left him there to bleed.

Now it happened that, upon the road,
a priest passed near; he saw the young man lying there,
but he just passed him by.

Then came a lawyer of business mind who had more than he
could spend.
He likewise ignored the man and went on the road he had been
on.

Then came a man both strong and kind,
and he put him on his back,
carried him to a nearby inn,
just a little way down the track .

He shared some of his food and left money for his keep.
And told the hotel owner,
"Get him well; I pay upkeep."

The man they call a Samaritan, it's the name those of kind,
who put others before themselves,
the poor, the drunk, the blind.

Now, youth today walk on The Way
to discover their own souls.
Whilst those of us towards the end
were letting go of our load.

Suffice to say, along The Way,
the poor, the lame, just beg.
While pilgrims on the Camino
see naught but what's ahead.

Santiago Travellers,
travelling the path,
doing their own thing,
walking the Camino Way
for the freedom it will bring.

Crossing New Horizons.

The way across the **Meseta** unfolds beneath vast and shifting skies, a landscape stretching out like an endless ocean with no shore in sight. This broad plain has a reputation that divides pilgrims—some dread its monotony, while others cherish its stillness and quiet truth. Yet the Meseta is not empty. It holds within it the living presence of great cities such as **Burgos** and **León,** where the sudden appearance of towering cathedrals feels almost surreal after days of horizon and sky. These sacred landmarks rise with a beauty that feels both grounding and otherworldly—anchors in a sea of earth and light. To the north, the rugged silhouette of the **Cordillera Cantábrica** cuts across the sky, a distant companion to the pilgrim's path.

Along the way, small desert flowers push through the dry soil, delicate and defiant, adding colour to the otherwise muted tones. There's a strange, almost dreamlike quality to it all—a sense of walking in a dream where time softens, and distance becomes something felt rather than measured.

The Meseta can disorient. Its sameness challenges the mind, and yet recent lines of planted trees offer both guidance and reassurance, gently leading pilgrims forward when the path seems to dissolve into the horizon. In this quiet vastness, the landscape invites reflection. Thoughts surface unbidden, memories drift in and out, and the boundary between the past and the present begins to blur.

There is something deeply contemplative here. The Meseta evokes echoes of medieval pilgrims who walked these same paths centuries before, their hopes and burdens carried across the same open ground. In this way, the experience becomes both spiritual and timeless—a merging of what has been, what is, and what may yet come.

And so, the Meseta draws from the pilgrim a kind of introspection that is as profound on the open plain as it is beneath the vaulted ceilings of the great cathedrals. It is not merely a crossing of land, but a crossing inward—a quiet, expansive journey through the soul itself.

The distant silhouette of the hills inspired the character of Don Quixote de la Mancha in a novel, the spirituality of St. Teresa, and the mystical notions of St. John of the Cross. Legend has it that Mohammad visited this desert too, as did St. James, but all of this—though inspiring for those who seek the spirit of these men—seems to a sceptical mind to be pure make-believe. Still, the monotony of crossing the desert served as a myriad of wilderness experiences for me like no other, for who am I to doubt the mystical magic of that Mesata for other wandering souls.

Venturing away from the hectic pace of a modern city, Burgos nonetheless has many fine sights, including museums, medieval art, and contemporary culture that far surpass those of cities of a similar size. Still, it was good to escape the urban landscape of Burgos and return once more to the peaceful Meseta, walking through a wheat field before the hope of final rains would come before the harvest. Onward past the healing springs of **San Bol**, where St. Anthony performed miracles healing pilgrims of the skin condition called, as previously mentioned, 'St. Anthony's fire." As a result of this crusade, the 11th-century order of St. Anthony earned a reputation for curing the disease by constantly plunging sufferers of that itchy, swollen skin condition into freezing waters during winter. I had mistakenly believed that my swollen feet and blisters might be cured by immersing my feet in cold water run-off from crops fed via aqueducts; the act only worsened my condition, since I had not taken into account that the water was full of chemicals to encourage crop growth. It has taken the better part of a decade and some to cure my ills from itchy, swollen outbreaks. A trial may work better sometimes, but not always.

The trail continued along paved roads and through villages that overlap the memory of my first and second Caminos on this same route. There was a strange familiarity in it all—as though time had folded in on itself, and I was walking not just forward, but through the echoes of who I had once been.

 On my first Camino, I was trying to release a lifetime of pain and suffering. I pushed myself relentlessly, almost as if the physical hardship might somehow match or purge what I carried. In truth, my body bore the cost of that effort. Each step felt like a punishment, each day an endurance. Looking back now, it may seem irrational—perhaps even reckless—but I sense it was necessary at that moment in my life. It was the only way I knew how to begin letting go.
The second crossing was no less difficult, though its trials came in a different form. Illness followed me like a shadow. Influenza drained what strength I had, and the rain—unceasing, cold, and heavy—soaked everything. Day blurred into night under grey skies, my clothes never dry, my body never warm. And yet, I endured. That is the quiet truth the

Camino reveals: that the human spirit is capable of far more than we believe. When the mind settles into acceptance—when there is no longer resistance, only movement forward—almost anything can be carried, and somehow, survived.

Now, walking this path again, there is less urgency, less struggle. The road is still long, the villages still worn by time, but I move through them differently. Not as a man fleeing his burdens, nor one simply trying to outlast suffering, but as someone who has come to understand that the journey was never about escaping pain—it was about learning how to walk with it, and eventually, beyond it.

As **Hontanas** came into sight, memories of my previous two stays there floated back to me; the abundance of clear, pure water was a blessing at mealtime. Entering the village hamlet, the 14th-century **Igelia de la Immaculada Concepción**, a beautiful church devoted to the Virgin Mary, towers over the small huts that have remained there for centuries.

A record of the town's history was entered into local records by an Italian pilgrim in 1670, who complained bitterly of the dangers posed by packs of wolves before his arrival in **Hontanas.** According to his account, these wolves were known to attack sheep under the cover of darkness and foul the nearby streams, creating both fear and hardship for those who lived along the Way.

The residents, in response, built strong fences around their huts and gathered their flocks each night, protecting them as best they could from the threat that lingered just beyond the edge of firelight. Even now, there remains a quiet local belief that it is unwise to walk the Camino in the early morning or late afternoon, when shadows lengthen, and the land feels more vulnerable to what may still roam unseen.

I took these stories with a grain of salt on my previous pilgrimages across that stark and open country. In all my journeys, I never saw a single wild dog—nor, for that matter, many sheep. Whether under the relentless heat of summer or the cold, soaking rains of another year, the land seemed empty of such dangers. Perhaps the conditions had something to do with it, or perhaps time itself had softened those older realities.

But I also know I was never inclined to dwell on such possibilities. I was not in the habit of manifesting anything that might interfere with the progress I was making. My focus remained forward—on the path, on the purpose, and on the quiet awareness of where I was in each moment. And in that awareness, the fears of the past seemed to fade into the distance, much like the horizon itself—always present, yet never quite within reach.

Memories drift back now of that long day's journey under the relentless weight of the noonday sun, walking beside the **Canal de Castilla,** then onward along the road through **Población de Campos** and on to **Revenga de Campos**—an eighteen-kilometre stretch from **Boadilla del Camino,** where I had stayed on my first pilgrimage.

It was hot, dry, and unrelenting. The dust clung to everything. There was no shade, no ready water, no food—only the long road ahead and the occasional oasis of the villages I've just named. It was a stretch that felt endless, with no turning back, and I walked it alone until I reached **Revenga.**

I remember it as a small albergue set quietly in that open land —almost like a mirage made real. A private room, good food, and a stillness that felt earned after the day's effort. Yet at that time, The Way held little sacred meaning for me. It was simply a road—long, unforgiving, and leading to what felt like nowhere. I walked it more as a solitary drifter than a pilgrim, with little thought for beauty or reflection.

I recall vaguely walking through Revenga on my second French Way of the Camino. My constant slogging through wild rain and boggy roadways took up most of my concentration and a sense of acceptance, with little else to think about. The bridge before that previous stay in the albergue, I do, for it was about six clicks away, where I had the wind carry me walking poles over the edge of the bridge and into an empty canyon some meters below. I had climbed down the wire rope with a hand towel to save me from metal cuts and rescued the poles below. I found my way along the canal to a ladder, wading in ankle-deep water, just enough to fill my boots, then up the concrete canal wall, and back to the bridge. I turn my head upwards to the sky and call to the universe: "And what was the point of that?" Oh, I could ask myself that again and again when I recall so many pointless incidents over my lifetime. The Camino taught so many lessons in patience and perseverance, and more patience. It was not just my journey that was at issue here. Yet, even then, the Camino had a way of placing stories in my path.

Over a simple meal in that refugio at Revenga, I met a Danish children's psychologist travelling with his son, an actor. The father spoke of something that lingered deeply with me—not in the moment perhaps, but in memory. He told of an old

Viking presence that would appear to him, carrying an iron sword, drawing him into dangerous situations that seemed to spill from imagination into the reality of his life and work.

Whether it was metaphor, memory, or something more, I could not say. But the man believed in it enough to carry a burden of his own—a symbolic act, taking that "iron weight" all the way to **Finisterre,** where many pilgrims go to cast off what they no longer wish to carry.

I remember thinking then, in my own quiet and detached way, that if I had borne such a weight—if I had felt that same shadow over my life—I too might have carried that sword to the edge of the world and thrown it into the sea. I do not know if he ever completed that journey as he intended. I hope he did.

Because looking back now, I see that even when the Way meant little to me, it was already at work—placing before me reflections of burden, release, and the quiet human need to lay something down at the end of a long road.

By the time I reached **Carrión de los Condes**, I felt quietly prepared—armed not just with the geography of the village, but with fragments of its history that seemed to linger in the air itself. One story in particular stayed with me: the legend of the one hundred Christian maidens demanded each year by the Moors. It is said that this cruel tribute was miraculously brought to an end when a wild herd of bulls descended upon the Moorish camp, scattering them and lifting the curse. Whether myth or memory, it carried the weight of a people's longing for deliverance.

Drawn deeper into the town's past, I made my way to **Iglesia de Santiago**—or rather, what remains of the original 12th-century structure, later rebuilt after the fire of 1845. Within its walls, history gave way to something more immediate and alive. I found myself among singing nuns and a gathering of young pilgrims, our voices rising together in joyful song. It was one of those rare moments on the Camino where time seems to dissolve—the past, present, and spirit all merging into a single, resonant memory that still echoes within.

Beyond the village lay the long, unbroken stretches of the ancient Roman road—those relentless, straight paths that test both body and mind. The 21-kilometre journey toward **Calzadilla de la Cueza** is one such passage, stark and unyielding. It was along this route that thoughts of the **Knights Templar** returned to me—guardians of pilgrims, bound by vows of protection and service. The Knights Templar were a medieval military order appointed by the pope who claimed great power as moneylenders and established the practice of letters of credit; the modern form of banking has its roots in this.

While the Templars were popular for over 200 years for their protection of citizens against the Moors in battle, and vagabonds and thieves, their reign came to an end when Grand Master Jacques de Molay was arrested in 1307 and burned at the stake for heresy and a variety of trumped-up charges. The order was disbanded in disgrace, but it was more political than actually wrong-doing. Many secret orders in modern-day Christianity preserve the Templars' workings and continue their duties on a simpler basis.

On those long days along the road, passing through countless villages and small hamlets, my mind would often drift back to my arrival in **Burgos**—a memory made all the richer by the company I kept.

I had met them earlier along the Way, in a quiet village café—two Spanish women whose warmth and spirit seemed to capture something of the Camino itself. We shared conversation as pilgrims do, easily and without expectation, bound by the road beneath our feet rather than the lives we had left behind. There was a lightness to that meeting, as though it existed outside of time.

By chance or design, we found ourselves walking into **Burgos** together. Their journey, they told me, would end there—for now. They spoke of returning the following year to complete what they had begun, their Camino unfolding in chapters rather than a single telling. There was something deeply fitting in that, as if the road itself had permitted them to pause, knowing it would call them back again.

And in time, through later communication, I learned that they had indeed returned, just as they had hoped—resuming their pilgrimage and carrying it through to its completion.

It is curious how such brief encounters can leave such a lasting imprint. On a path where so many faces come and go, some remain with you—not as passing strangers, but as part of the story, you continue to walk.

We had shared only a single day, yet the bond felt far deeper—as though the Camino had briefly woven our paths together with quiet intention. I was both mentally and physically captivated by one of them in particular. There was a lightness to her, even in struggle, and I came to call her my *dancing queen*.

She suffered greatly on that long, punishing day—the blisters, the relentless heat, the creeping dehydration that tested us all. And yet she carried on with quiet resilience, making her all the more remarkable. By chance, we both stayed that night at the main albergue in **Burgos,** sharing a small room with other weary pilgrims, each of us retreating into our own exhausted silence.

Like Ships in the Night.

As was my habit, I rose early to take to the road before dawn. When I said goodbye, she reached out, held my hand gently, and offered a soft, fleeting smile before rolling over, returning to sleep. It was a simple moment—almost nothing at all—yet it lingered.

I didn't realise until later that she had slipped a note into my knapsack. It was somewhere further along the Way that I discovered it, and with the help of an albergue proprietor, her words were brought to life in English: *"Thank you for being so kind to me on a dreadful day. I kiss you."*

That note became the beginning of a quiet correspondence that lasted for two years—letters, messages, a thread of connection stretching across distance and time.

Like so many things born on the Camino, it was not meant to last forever. Gradually, almost imperceptibly, our communication faded. What remained were the occasional birthday wishes, a passing acknowledgment on social media—like ships in the night, once close, now drifting on separate tides. And yet, the memory endured—not as something lost, but as something complete in its own fleeting, beautiful way.

I, for a fleeting moment, held the note to my heart, but destiny would all too soon force me to surrender. Indeed, as equally as the crucifix around my neck back then, the one that Brother John of the Brothers of Mother Teresa had bestowed upon me. At the time, I was caught up in the search for the beauty of the foreign maid, in my own desperate plea for love.

Is it the sound I'm hearing in the trees,
Do I see you in the falling leaves?

Maybe it's the sweetness of the breeze,
the feel of sand between my toes.

We did our mating in some distant past,
Life was always splendid in the grass,
Now feelings are faded memories,
And nothing ever lasts for long.

Is it the woman cradled in my arms,
the warmth of her constant charms,
maybe it's the child upon my lap,
that sense of innocence.

Oh! Love,
Come back into my room,
and take away these blues.

Did I see you in the corner of my eye?
the shadow of the bird flying by,
the warmth of the sun upon my face,
maybe now in a fading cloud.

Do I see you in the smiling face?
The parade of the human race,
maybe it's in some isolation,
On some foreign plain.

Did I see you on the road somewhere?
Was it a gentle hand upon my back,
maybe it's the burden of the load,
When I look back.

Now I am here out upon the track,
walking with my knapsack on my back,
taking the rough with the smooth,

looking for the love that I once knew.

Oh! love,
Come back into my room,
and take away these blues.

Crossing the Meseta, treading ancient Roman paths and climbing long, patient hills, I walked a landscape stamped with the memory of medieval pilgrims and modern-day seekers alike. At times, I would catch sight of the weathered walls of **Mansilla de las Mulas,** standing as they have for centuries, while I moved through it all, absorbed in the daily grind of an overloaded backpack.

Back then, it did not seem to matter much—whether under the harsh blaze of the summer sun or, on my second journey, through the mud and slush of spring rains. The long roads stretching from **Burgos** to **León** carried me through a chain of small villages and larger towns, each different in character, yet bound by a shared rhythm of pilgrimage that I slowly became part of.

Looking back now, I realise how much I adapted—how the hardships became normal. Blistered feet were no longer a problem; they were just an expected part of the day. Hunger was managed. Sleep was uncertain in noisy albergues. The weight of the pack, the heat, the occasional dehydration—all of it folded into a routine that defined life on the Camino.
It became a quiet acceptance. We moved together as a loose community of pilgrims, drawn forward by something not entirely understood. There was always a sense of a destination, a magnetic pull toward something beyond the horizon, though few of us could clearly define what that was.

And yet, it was on those long desert crossings that something began to shift within me.

After a time, the suffering seemed to loosen its grip. In its place came a kind of stillness—and from that stillness, creativity began to emerge. Thoughts, reflections, fragments of meaning surfaced as I walked. What had once been endurance slowly became observation, then expression.

Through diary entries, I began to record these moments—not fully understanding their importance at the time, but sensing they mattered. Seeds planted in the dust of the Meseta, waiting for another time, another version of myself, to return and make sense of them. As I do now.

And yet I wonder if I have truly learned the meaning of surrender. Endurance is one thing. You proved that long ago—through heat, illness, exhaustion, and the sheer repetition of putting one foot in front of the other. Mental conditioning is another—to let go, to loosen the grip, to stop fighting what is. But surrender… real surrender… that is something deeper, and far less tangible.

It isn't about giving up the world, nor is it about no longer feeling its pressures. And it's certainly not about becoming passive or detached from life. Surrender, in its truest sense, is the quiet release of resistance. It is no longer trying to force myself into shapes that were never meant for me—the square peg and the round hole I speak of. You, dear reader, already see it. You're on the edge of it.

To fully surrender would not feel dramatic. It wouldn't arrive with some grand revelation or final moment of victory. It would feel… simpler than that. Lighter. As though something I've been carrying for a very long time has quietly slipped from my shoulders—like when I put my backpack down, the relief always came, and at first I didn't even notice the exact moment it happened.

There would be less questioning of where I now "fit," and more acceptance of where I simply am in the moment. Less effort in becoming, and more ease in being. And what would I do with my time then? Most likely, not much differently on the surface.
I would continue to take a daily walk, still write, still observe. But the energy behind it would change. There would be no need to prove, no need to resolve, no need to escape anything. I wouldn't be walking to outrun pain, nor writing to make sense of it. I would be doing both because they are natural expressions of who I am. I therefore conclude that surrender doesn't remove purpose—it refines it. It turns effort into presence. Striving for awareness. Burden into something that no longer needs to be carried. And perhaps the quiet truth is this: the fact that I am asking the question means I am already living it, at least in part.

The path to freedom within is not fully arrived—perhaps no one ever is—but no longer where I once was pursuing to be. Just… walking the line between holding on and letting go, much like the Camino itself.
So after crossing so many borders of physical, mental, and spiritual striving on Masada, it was time for rest and awe upon arriving in **León.**

León arrives on the Camino almost like a threshold. After the long, testing openness of the Meseta, the city feels alive in a different way—both grounding and expansive. For many pilgrims, it marks a shift. Not just geographically, but inwardly. The long plains begin to give way to something richer, greener, more varied… and often, something within begins to change as well. On both my French Camino journeys, it was Léon where I took two days out to contemplate the old medieval world, but one street from its border, from the old, a 21st-century city emerges with its modernity, fast pace and vibrance. It was with that experience that I was ready to face the real world and, just as easily, drift into the surreal world of history and mythology, all by crossing a street.

At the heart of this great city stands the magnificent **León Cathedral**—a structure of light as much as stone. Its vast stained-glass windows seem to dissolve the walls themselves, filling the interior with colour and silence. After days or weeks of dust, heat, or rain, stepping inside can feel almost unreal, like entering a different dimension of the same journey.
Not far away is the **Basilica of San Isidoro**, quieter, older, holding centuries of history in its thick walls and painted ceilings. Where the cathedral lifts the spirit upward, San Isidoro draws it inward.

León is also a place of pause. A place where many pilgrims rest, reflect, and take stock of what has already been walked. The body recovers a little. The mind catches up. The journey so far begins to settle into memory, even as the road ahead still calls.

For me, it may not have been just a city, but a crossing point between different versions of myself—the one who endured,

the one who questioned, and the one who is now beginning to understand. León doesn't ask anything of you.
It simply stands there—ancient, luminous, and still—waiting for you to notice what has changed within since you last arrived.

It was the old world that I was drawn to more than the modern vibrance and culture of this fair city. I lived it. loved it like it was my last days on earth, and in the corners of my mind, it sometimes to this day appears that way. For there always I was drawn back from the shadows of my mind to the light of that luminous stand, the Cathedral, always the Cathedral. The fortress of sacred beauty between two worlds. The stained glass windows of the Cathedral and the reality of the light that penetrated them. It was always the light that had drawn me toward those stained glass windows, luminous and alive. Within them lived countless motifs and sacred icons, as well as stories of suffering and resurrection. But it was not the images alone that moved me—it was the light that transformed them. The sunlight, breaking through the glass, gave life to what would otherwise remain silent and obscure.
It was the Light. Without that light, the shadows upon the windows would reveal very little of what truly lay within them. And so it was, day after day on the Camino, that I began to see myself in much the same way.

There were days when I walked in shadow—when the weight of memory, of loss, and of questions unanswered pressed heavily upon me. In those moments, I felt like the darkened glass: full of form, full of story, yet without clarity or meaning. I carried within me fragments of suffering, of love, of things broken and things longed for—but I could not always see them as whole. Then, without warning, the light would come. Just as it so suddenly shone through the panels of glass, shooting the colours of the rainbow within the darkness of the cathedral, and telling a story for the viewer in every glass panel.

Sometimes, on my trudging through it all, the light of my existence arrived in the simplest of ways—a stranger's kindness, a shared meal, the rhythm of footsteps on an endless path, or the quiet stillness of a village church. And suddenly, everything within me seemed illuminated. The same fragments of my life that once felt heavy and disjointed began to reveal a deeper pattern—one not defined by suffering alone, but by endurance, by grace, and by something quietly resembling resurrection, like the light on the glass panels in the **Cathedral of Leon.**

I came to understand that the journey was never about escaping the shadows, but about learning to wait for the light. For without the light, I could not truly see myself. And perhaps that is the quiet truth the Camino offers—not that we are broken pieces wandering without meaning, but that we are, like those ancient windows, waiting for the light to pass through us… so that our story may finally be seen.

We walk the Camino carrying our stories as if they are burdens, as if they are things to be fixed or hidden. Yet perhaps they are neither. Perhaps they are simply waiting—for the right light, at the right moment, to pass through them.
I remember standing there for a long time, not moving, not thinking—only watching as the light shifted with the passing day, reshaping everything it touched. And I began to

understand then that the journey I was on was not about outrunning the shadows within me. It was about learning to stand still long enough for the light to find me. For without it, I could not truly see who I was.

And perhaps that is the quiet miracle of places like this—of the Camino itself. Not that they change us, but that they reveal us… illuminated, not despite our fractures, but because of them. A memory of a wise man, Emerson, who once wrote that we should *"write it on your heart that every day is the best day in the year."*

Then my mind turned to the countless pilgrims who had walked this path across the ages—long before my own footsteps ever touched the dust of the Way—some order out of Chaos.

We are but shattered pieces, scattered across the quiet landscape of our lives—fragments of love, of loss, of fleeting moments we barely understood as they passed through us. Each piece carries its own story, some we hold close, others we try to leave behind, as though they never belonged to us at all.

And yet, none of it is wasted.

We are like shards of a mirror in the void—a reflection of the universe itself. Broken, incomplete, yet capable of catching the light. Like the stained glass of **León Cathedral,** it is through our fractures that the light passes, revealing forms, colours, and truths far greater than we could perceive alone. Individually, we are jagged, fragmentary—shadows of something beyond our comprehension.

But together, across time and space, our pieces create a universal reflection: a mosaic of human experience, of suffering and joy, of shadow and illumination. Fragile, yet resilient. Fleeting, yet eternal.

And in that reflection, the light finds its way into the darkest scenes—revealing not only what has been broken, but what endures. What persists. What, against all odds, shines.

I was in the shadow of the hilltop now. The light behind me was thinning, stretched long across the path as the day began its gentle descent toward evening.

A Grail for Me.

 I had already trodden through the quiet ambience of tiny stone villages—**Astorga, Valdeviejas, Murias de Rechivaldo, Santa Catalina**. Each one is a small milestone on the map, yet a world unto itself. Clusters of stone and silence, humble doorways, fading paint, and the faint echo of footsteps from pilgrims long forgotten.

The road sloped ever upward, as though urging me onward through the last twenty kilometres of the day. By the time I reached **Rabanal del Camino,** the sun was leaning low toward the horizon. Warm light washed over the village's stone walls, turning them gold for a fleeting moment before dusk reclaimed them. There, I crossed paths with two Italian pilgrims—lovers in their lives, and lovers of life itself.

Their laughter carried through the evening air, light and effortless, as though sorrow had never found them. We shared coffee, conversation, and that peculiar intimacy that belongs only to strangers who meet on the Road.

For a while, time seemed to hold still—three pilgrims, three stories, bound briefly together in the fading light.

Eventually, they rose, smiling warmly, and bid me a fond farewell. And as the shadows lengthened, I turned toward my destination—**Foncebadón.** A village perched on the edge of the world, waiting for me at the crest of the hill. I turned for one last wave to the Italian pilgrims as they disappeared into the sunset, silhouettes hand in hand, climbing the last steep stretch toward their own resting place for the night.

The air grew cooler. The path quieted. And with each step, I felt the solitude deepen—not as loneliness, but as a kind of belonging. Here, in the embrace of the mountains, in the shadow of the coming night, the Camino held me gently in its silence. The shadows stretched long across the path, softening the sharp edges of the stones beneath my feet. The mountains held the light a little longer than the valleys, but even they could not stop the slow retreat of the sun. I had fallen behind my young band of brothers, and the young German rock musician had told me the albergue at the top had only a few beds, but he would do his best to hold one for me. There was a strange comfort in being an hour behind—a space where no one hurried me, where the world seemed to breathe, but I was already out of water. It didn't seem to bother me that much, and as I rounded a bend in the mountain terrain, I felt the solitude deepen—not as loneliness, but as a kind of belonging. Here, in the embrace of the mountains, in the shadow of the coming night, the Camino held me gently in its silence.

I continued along the fading light until I came across a water trough meant for livestock, a simple stone basin with a tap running steadily into it. I drank my fill, let the cold water revive me, and refilled my container. For a short moment, I even considered camping there for the night. The quietness of the place, the soft murmur of the running water, and the solitude held a strange appeal. But after a brief rest, hunger nudged me onward. Perhaps, I thought, if I pushed on, there might still be an evening meal available at the albergue in **Foncebadón.**

Eventually, the old albergue came into view—its silhouette rough and ancient against the last light of day. I stepped inside through a narrow passage that opened into a dim nave, where long wooden tables were crowded with pilgrims waiting eagerly to be fed. The air buzzed with the low hum of voices, fatigue, and anticipation.

Behind a small makeshift counter was the kitchen—if one could call it that. A long-haired, wild-looking Spaniard emerged from behind it, a cat draped casually across his shoulders as if part of his daily uniform. Beside him, his off-sider stood over a massive paella pan—large enough, it seemed, to feed an army of hungry pilgrims. The aroma filled the room like incense.

I approached the Spaniard and asked if he had a spare bed for the night. Without even looking up, he waved me away.

"No beds left," he muttered. My heart sank. Then I mentioned that the German musician had reserved one for me. At once, his head snapped up. "Ah! You are the Australian!" he said, pointing a finger at me with theatrical certainty. "There *is* a bed for you."

Relief washed over me like a blessing. The unwashed proprietor directed me outside to the rear courtyard, where a covered platform stood above what was an animal shelter. It was crude, open to the night air, and hardly luxurious—but it was a place to rest. A roof, a mat, and shelter from the wind. That was enough.

Like so many others that night, I unrolled my floor mat, set down my pack, and let the day's weight slip away. I washed quickly in a nearby basin—cold water, sharp and cleansing—and made my way back to join the throng awaiting the evening meal.

On the way, I crossed paths with the German rock musician—the one who had secured my bed. In that instant, gratitude overwhelmed me. Without thinking, I dropped to one knee and kissed his foot, as an apostle might for his lord. It was dramatic, foolish even, but entirely sincere. I had vowed earlier that if he found me a bed, I would kiss his feet in thanks. And so I did. To my surprise, he simply laughed—a rich, musical laugh—and lifted me back to my feet with both hands.

In that strange and sacred moment, beneath the rising stars of **Foncebadón,** I felt the Camino's unspoken truth again: On this road, we carry each other—sometimes with words, sometimes with kindness, and sometimes with gestures absurd and holy all at once.

I recall now—almost with a wry smile—that this old albergue was closed down just two weeks later. It hadn't passed the health inspection. And looking back, I can't say I was surprised.

The place had a chaotic charm, held together more by spirit than by structure. The cat in the kitchen, the enormous paella pan seasoned by generations of unknown hands, the makeshift sleeping platforms over an old animal shelter—none of it would ever have satisfied an inspector's checklist. Yet for us pilgrims that night, it was perfect in its own way. A place on the edge of the world, raw and real, untouched by the neatness of modern life. A refuge offered by people who cared more about feeding hungry walkers than about regulations or appearances.

There was something beautifully human about it—imperfect, flawed, unsanitised…and yet filled with warmth and generosity. Perhaps that is why I remember it so clearly. Not because of the conditions, but because of the connection. Because of the laughter, the shared meal, the gratitude, and the kindness of a musician who saved me a bed. Because, in its roughness, it reminded me of what the Camino truly is: a journey shaped not by comfort, but by the unexpected grace we meet along the way. Even if the building itself couldn't survive a health inspection, the memory of that night survives in me—untouched, unbroken, and somehow more sacred for all its imperfections.

As I had mentioned, **three magic moments** outlasted that night. The first was waking to find the two Italian pilgrims sleeping beside me on the thin mats laid out across the wooden platform. There was something comforting about their presence—familiar strangers whose laughter and warmth from the evening before had carried over into the quiet hours of dawn. For a moment, I simply lay there, listening to the soft breaths of pilgrims rising and falling around me, like waves on a calm shore.

The second memory arrived by way of the cat—the same long-haired creature that had padded across the kitchen counter the night before. Seeing it again in the morning light brought back another moment from earlier on the Camino:

a courtyard meal interrupted by a full clowder of cats that descended upon me from all directions. I have never been a cat person, but the Camino has a way of presenting us with what we would rather avoid. Sometimes lessons come in uncomfortable shapes, and we may never know exactly what

they were meant to teach us. Later, as we prepared for the day's walk, I spoke with the Italians about this—about how the Camino nudges us, challenges us, softens us. It reminded me, too, of actress Shirley MacLaine and her account of the Camino. In her book, she described her fear of dogs—
and the wild dogs of Foncebadón that roamed in packs and attacked pilgrims, or so the stories said. But I had never seen anything like that on my previous Caminos. Most of the dogs I encountered simply lay wherever they could find a sliver of shade, panting quietly, exhausted by the heat—hardly the beasts of legend.

To prove the point, I had even approached two growling dogs behind a wire fence on my way up the mountain. Instead of fear, I spoke gently to them—soft words, slow steps. Their growling faded into low whimpers of confusion. They came closer, curious, peering at me with tilted heads as if trying to understand why I offered no fear, no threat. And in that simple moment, I realised they were just as tired, just as vulnerable, just as bewildered by the world as the rest of us. They didn't bother me after that. That was the real lesson: On the Camino, even the creatures we fear soften when met with kindness. And sometimes, the shadows we carry are far larger than the things that cast them.

And **The Third miracle.** Around midnight, I rose and joined the little band of brothers sitting on a bench overlooking the valley below. The German rock musician had found an old guitar at the albergue and began strumming a few rock-and-roll tunes. Then he shifted into a beautiful ballad of his own making, and it brought to mind a poem I had written on the train from Paris to St Jean about my grandfather. I told him about it, and he asked me to read it to him. I rummaged in my backpack for the rough notes and recited the piece under the soft glow of the night.

The German rock musician had not forgotten my poem. I thought nothing more of it—until I returned to Australia. Out of the blue, he emailed me asking for the lyrics so he could set them to music for his next album. At the time, it had no chorus, so I sent him another poem instead, and he recorded that one. Then, as if stirred by the Camino itself, the chorus for my *Boundary Rider* poem came to me. I sent him the finished piece, and he recorded that song for his next album as well.

That night on the mountain set me on a new course of creative pursuit. The books I have written, the albums I have produced, all started with just that one song.
It took me a long time to understand why that night in Foncebadón became a turning point. On the surface, it was simple enough: a German rock musician with an old guitar, a valley wrapped in silence, a few weary pilgrims sharing the last warmth of the day. But something far deeper moved beneath it — something ancient, something personal, something that had been waiting inside me since childhood.

When the musician asked me to read the poem about my grandfather, the words came alive again. I felt as though I were not simply reading but *returning* — stepping back into the presence of the man who had shaped my early life more profoundly than I ever recognised. My grandfather had been the first storyteller I ever knew, the first voice that showed me how a simple tale could become a doorway into another world.

He narrated the land, the horses, the storms, and the quiet moments beside a fire. He taught me that a story was not just a sequence of events but a vessel for truth, warmth, and wonder. For a boy who felt abandoned, it was my grandfather who gave me the companionship of imagination — an invisible friend who never left.

It was as if a dormant part of me stood upright again: the child who had once believed stories could shape the world suddenly remembered that he *could* shape them. What I thought was a poem became the seed for a song, and the song became the seed for a new creative life.

Looking back, it was never really the guitarist, nor the albergue, nor even the Camino itself that sparked my transformation. *It was love.* The love of a grandfather whose stories carried me through childhood like a quiet lantern in the dark. The love that came rushing back the moment his memory was spoken into the cold air of that mountain village. The love that reminded me who I was before the world asked me to be anything else.

And so, without fully realising it, I stepped into a new chapter — one where the pen, the melody, and the journey became my companions. Every book, every song, every creative step since then traces its beginning back to him.

Fate placed me on that bench at midnight, but love placed the words in my hands.

Oh! I've been a boundary rider.

On the wild New England Range

Round up ranging- cattle

Driven more across the plains

Oh! I learned to live the bush way
When I was just a kid,
camping out with my ole granddad,
cutting timbers, what he did.

I've had my share of hard times,
I've had my fill of pain,
If I had my time back over,
probably do it all again.

Killing dingoes when in danger,
cooking rabbit to survive,
staying warm at night, log fire,
sleeping out when I was five.

Well, I crossed the barren desert,
and I tramped the hills alone,
made it through some swollen rivers,
wild dust storms and chilly snows.

> " Hear the thunder on the mountain,
> It's the brumbies on the run,
> see the murder of the black crows,
> as they greet the morning sun.
>
> Feel the gentle chill of first light,
> Tea and damper's almost done,
> breaking camp, we long to start,
> Saddle up for a boundary run."
>
> Well, my granddad was a drover,
> cross the country he did roam,
> seeking out his heart's companion,
> where he found his heart and home.

Boxed in tents for Jimmy Sharman,
tried to earn a decent quid,
carried swag across the Darling,
seeking work, that's what he did.

He cut timber on the north coast,
drove cattle on the plain,
panned for gold in old Kalgoorlie,
strut the boards and sang on stage,

Once he sat on his verandah,
telling stories to grandkids,
of the life he'd left behind him,
and the things that he once did.

So I sing this song for granddad,
In my heart, he will remain,
cause he was a boundary rider,
On the wild New England Range.

Letting Go.

The short climb from Foncebadón to **Cruz de Ferro** on that first Camino was made in the soft dawning light, my little band of brothers walking beside me in a kind of sacred hush. As we ascended, I thought of the saintly hermit who once lived in these hills, the man who took an ancient pagan *titum pole* — a relic of beliefs long older than Christianity — and transformed it by placing a simple crucifix at its peak. That pole, rising above a mountain of stones left by pilgrims through the centuries, felt like a bridge between worlds: the old and the new, the pagan and the Christian, the private burden and the universal longing for release.

And so we continued onward, lighter not because the burden had vanished, but because **The Way** had taken some of its weight into itself. The pathway drew us ever onward toward what we did not know. That is the truth of the Camino: you walk forward into mystery, step by step, sometimes with purpose, sometimes with nothing but faith in the next bend of the trail.

On that first Camino, the memory is all heat — the relentless downhill trudge under a blistering sun. On the second, it was the opposite: a deluge of rain that seemed to fall without mercy. Yet in both, the same truth lingered — *the Way humbles you.* It strips you back until only the essential remains.

The little hamlets slipped by like fragments from some ancient dream: **El Acebo, Riego de Ambrós, Molinaseca** — each one a whisper from the past, each one a step deeper into the story of the land and the story of myself. I remember the winding bridge leading toward **Ponferrada,** and then the sudden sight of the great **Templar castle**, standing sentinel over the town like a guardian from a long-forgotten age. Beyond it lay the lush pastures of **El Bierzo**, tucked into its mountain cradle. I can still taste the cured meats of those small villages, the sweetness of cherries offered by villagers whose generosity was as rich as the soil they lived upon.

And then came **Villafranca del Bierzo**, with its shaded garden beside the Iglesia de Santiago. I remember standing before the **Puerta del Perdón — the Gate of Forgiveness**. It stirred something old in me, something familiar: the long chain of sorrows I carried through life, decades of grief strung together like a rosary I had prayed too often. Yet not all memories were sorrowful.

In the rosary of my childhood, there had been joyful mysteries too — glimmers of innocence, wonder, and grace. I did not fully understand this then, not on that first Camino. But a flash of foresight touched me: that years later, on my second pilgrimage, I would kneel at **Fátima** and feel those mysteries return to me with unexpected tenderness. For now, though, it was just a brief memory — a whisper from the past threading itself through the present as I walked. The downward slopes toward Villafranca seemed endless. By then, I had lost sight of my young band of brothers. My weary soul, torn feet, and the relentless descent got the better of me on that first Camino. Somewhere along the way, I must have stepped off the well-worn pilgrim track and followed the gravel path of the old highway — a shortcut no longer much used. By the time I realised it, I was somehow ahead of my companions, walking alone into a small, half-forgotten village. I passed an old mill, its wheel silent and dark, and a weathered wooden olive press.

Flash from the past of a similar scene- the village of my childhood.

The path curved past a simple albergue, little more than a ranch-style house, modest and unassuming. What drew my attention were the paintings on its exterior walls — curious pieces of folk art, almost naïve in their simplicity. One showed a young Jesus, not the solemn Christ of cathedrals, but a boyish figure laughing over a game of cards with **São António de Padua** — the saint the Portuguese hold close to their hearts. I recognised him instantly.

St Anthony had been my quiet companion for as long as I could remember — the patron of lost causes, the finder of lost things. He had belonged originally to the Augustinian order before renouncing it for the Franciscans. A scholar, a preacher in Bologna, Toulouse, Montpellier, and Padua… yet he abandoned the cloistered life of a professor to become a wandering pilgrim, travelling through France, Spain, and Italy. That is why I always felt a kinship with him.

In my own life, I had abandoned old forms of belief, letting go of the rigid structures of religion and stepping instead into something more fluid — what one might simply call *spirituality*. Yet St Anthony remained with me. To this day, when I lose something, I call upon him, and almost without exception, the missing thing returns.

That small miracle has never failed me. It is the one thread of my childhood faith that I still hold onto with reverence.

But as for that wall painting — Jesus and St Anthony playing cards like two friends passing time on a warm afternoon — I never did learn its story. Perhaps the artist knew a local legend, or perhaps it was simply a moment of whimsy, captured by someone who saw no harm in imagining a prophet and a saint as ordinary men.

Whatever its meaning, it made me pause on my weary descent toward **Villafranca.** In that unexpected glimpse of sacred playfulness, I sensed again the curious ways the universe speaks when the road is long, and the traveller is tired.

Leaving Villafranca, the path wound through the valley, the mountains rising on either side like guardians watching over the weary pilgrim. The **El Bierzo** region unfolded in its lush beauty, vineyards and orchards giving way to quiet farmhouses and patches of forest where the silence seemed almost holy.

Then came the long approach to **O Cebreiro** — a climb that tests not only the body but also the will. On that first Camino, every step felt like a negotiation with pain. My legs burned, my feet were torn, and the mountain seemed to rise endlessly before me. But O Cebreiro has a way of rewarding the weary.

As the climb steepened and the air thinned, I found myself surrounded by mist — that ethereal Galician fog that appears without warning and wraps the world in white. It was as if I had stepped into another realm, somewhere halfway between heaven and earth.

When I finally reached the top, the ancient stone village emerged like something carved out of legend. The **pallozas** — round, thatched houses older than memory — stood solemn and silent in the mist. The **Iglesia de Santa María Real**, one of the oldest churches on the Camino, waited like a guardian of a thousand pilgrim stories.

I entered the church and sat in the dim light, the air heavy with centuries of prayer. Something deep within me loosened. Perhaps it was exhaustion, or altitude, or the weight of the kilometres behind me — but I felt, for a moment, the quiet presence of those who had walked before me, each carrying burdens of their own. In that silence, I understood something simple but profound: *The Camino does not erase your pain. It transforms it.*

And as I rested there in that ancient village nestled in the arms of the mountains, I felt the first stirrings of that transformation. It is now being recalled what it was to me then, but has ever since lingered within me.

The mist held **O Cebreiro** in its ghostly embrace as dawn crept over the mountain. I stepped out from the shelter of stone walls into a quiet that felt older than memory. Galicia was before me, now—land of green mountains, legends, miracles, and shadows—and I felt, without understanding why, that I had crossed an invisible threshold. The Camino changed here. So did I. In the stillness of the morning, the air carried something different—an ancient presence that whispered beneath the low clouds. **Galicia,** unlike the dry plains behind me, felt enchanted. The history here was not only Christian but had roots far deeper: **Celtic myth, Roman settlement, pagan rites,** the old stories of witches—"meigas"—whose presence the locals still acknowledge with a shrug and a knowing smile.

I had read once that in Galicia, there is a saying: "Eu non creo nas meigas, pero habelas, hainas." *I don't believe in witches, but yes, they exist.*

As I tightened the straps of my pack and set out on the steep descent toward **Triacastela,** I felt that strange mixture of Christianity and folklore—the very fabric of the Iberian Peninsula—brush against me like a chill draft.

For this was the land where the story of **St James** was said to have taken root. According to legend, he came here long before the great cathedral existed, preaching to villagers and fishermen, urging them to follow a new path in a land still shaped by the old gods. Some embraced him. Others resisted. But the myth endured—woven through these forests, these valleys, these rough-hewn tracks.

Leaving the stone village behind, I followed the rocky path that wound sharply downward. The trail was slick from the night's dew, and more than once I had to steady myself with my poles. Below me, layers of green folded into one another like waves. The scent of wet grass and pine drifted upward, and between breaks in the fog, clusters of houses appeared— dark roofs, grey stone walls, smoke curling from chimneys as families woke to the quiet rhythm of mountain life. My feet, battered from days of ascent, felt every stone.

The descent was a different kind of endurance—a slow surrender of altitude and ego. The first hamlets I entered felt like worlds suspended between eras. **Padornelo. Fonfría. O Biduedo.** Tiny clusters of homes where life had hardly changed for centuries. Chickens clucked through the lanes, dogs lifted sleepy heads as I passed, and older women swept their front steps while eyeing the solitary pilgrim with curiosity and caution.

Some still believed in the power of the old ways—charms against the evil eye, whispered prayers against misfortune, quiet offerings at roadside shrines. Christianity here was layered atop something older, like a fresco painted over another painting whose colours still bled faintly through.
I felt it all around me: the **syncretic faith** that defined these mountains, the coexistence of **ritual and superstition**, the sense that saints and spirits were never very far away.

As the trail grew steeper, my knees shook with every descent, and my mind drifted between the physical struggle and the inner landscape. This stretch of the Camino seemed designed to remind pilgrims that progress was always bought at a price. By midday, the mist thinned, giving way to brilliant clarity. I stopped near a wayside fountain, dipping my hands into the cold mountain water, letting the sting of it bring me back to myself. Below me lay the vast valley leading toward Triacastela—a tapestry of farms, fields, and forests stitched together by narrow stone tracks. By late afternoon, the spire of Triacastela came into view. The town—named after the three fortresses that once watched over the valley—felt like a gentle landing after the punishing descent.

I crossed a small bridge and entered its quiet streets, feeling both relief and a lingering sense of the unseen. **Galicia** had already worked some kind of transformation in me. The mix of myth, Christianity, pagan residue, and the legend of St James had awakened something half-buried in my own story: the awareness that we are shaped not only by belief, but by all the narratives we carry—sacred, personal, ancestral.

I found a bench in the fading light and set down my pack. As pilgrims trickled in from the trail, I felt again the unity of the journey—strangers walking the same steps, each carrying burdens visible and invisible. And somewhere in the back of my mind, the old Galician saying murmured once more:
I don't believe in witches… but yes, they exist.

In this land of mist and miracles, I began to understand that the Camino was not merely a physical road but a landscape of the soul—where the old and the new, the ancient and the modern, faith and doubt, sorrow and hope walk side by side.
Some say the Camino was a pagan pilgrimage long before it became a Christian one. A road of stars pointing toward the end of the world. A journey to confront one's shadow, to walk into mystery, to lay burdens down. You wondered, not for the first time, whether you were walking west to reach **Santiago**…or walking west to find the part of yourself you had abandoned somewhere long ago. Either way, the land was guiding you. For sure, though, I had long concluded The Camino always does.
On my first journey of *The Way*, I entered Triacastela not alone, but with one of my little band of brothers—Young by name, youthful in spirit. We had slipped out before dawn, chasing the cool of the early morning and the quiet that only the first light can give a pilgrim. We walked ahead of the others without a plan or strategy, simply following the rhythm of our boots and the easy friendship that forms when men share a common road.
It was Young who suggested the road less travelled, the long curve toward **Sarria,** drawn as much by curiosity as by the promise of boiled octopus—*pulpo*, the pride of Galicia. The

alternate route added nearly thirty kilometres to the stage, a detour most sensible pilgrims avoided. But something in us—some mix of hunger, mischief, and the thrill of taking a path less trodden—pulled us down the valley instead of across the ridge. That road wound through chestnut forests so old they seemed to hold conversations with themselves. Shafts of sunlight pierced the canopy like whispered blessings, and the river sang a gentle accompaniment at our side as we descended toward Samos.

I remember the taste of the octopus still—soft, salt-kissed, brushed with paprika and olive oil. Food is never just food on the Camino; it becomes part of the day's sacrament. After eating, we bathed in the clear, cold stream that ran over smooth stones. The shock of the water brought a fierce aliveness, a sense of being a child again in a world without demands. Then came the **Benedictine Monastery of Samos** — its ancient walls rising with quiet dignity, as though it did not need to impress anyone. Those stones had seen centuries of pilgrims come and go, had absorbed prayers whispered in a hundred languages, and carried them forward into the next generation.
I remember standing in its shadow, humbled by the weight of time, knowing that everything I feared and longed for was not new under the sun.

By mid-afternoon, Young left me. He believed, rightly or wrongly, that our other brothers had taken the main track toward Barbadelo, and he set off to find them. His departure left the valley quieter. I continued alone, climbing the long slope to rejoin the central route. By then, I had already carried a heavy pack for 700 kilometres—too heavy, of course, as most first-time pilgrims do. Pride and fear make fools of us all in those early days. But somewhere along the way, I had shed five kilos of unnecessary burden, and in doing so had unknowingly begun the real work: shedding the heaviness I'd been carrying on the inside. So the climb didn't trouble me. What mattered was the rhythm—walk, pause, breathe, notice. I sang songs to myself, old ones and ones I made up on the spot. I composed poems. I stopped often to peel off my boots and let my feet cool in the wind. I wrote in my journal, capturing the moments as though doing so might allow me to hold the pilgrim I was becoming. The second journey, years later, was not so different. The route remained the same, but I was not. This time, there was no lingering, no long pauses by the river. I had learned to keep on keeping on. The heat was unforgiving—extreme, relentless—and the 41 kilometres that day tested even the strongest resolve. Yet I found that whether in the searing dry or the cold wet of earlier pilgrimages, it made little difference to me anymore. I had adapted. I had become a rover, a pilgrim not just in distance but in identity— one searching for meaning, for truth, for surrender.

An Ode of Remembrance.

Somewhere between the high mountains and the Galician forests, the Camino had taught me a lesson that no teacher, priest, or philosopher ever had: When you walk long enough, when you hurt long enough, when you break open just enough, the road begins to walk you. And from that moment on, everything changes.

As **Galicia** opened before me, with its moss-draped stones and ancient lanes sunk deep below the fields like green tunnels, I sensed again that old whisper that this land carries—a whisper older than Christianity, older even than Rome. The land is the **Iberian Peninsula,** after all—a place woven from stories of witches and spirits, where the old religion had danced beside the new for centuries. The people here had long believed in signs, in protection from the unseen, in the thinness of the veil between this world and whatever lies beneath it. Even as Christianity spread through Spain, it did so by braiding itself around the older roots, not tearing them out.

I wonder, then, that this region held fast to the memory that **St. James himself—Santiago**—had preached here, that he had walked these riverbanks, spoken to farmers and fishermen, offered them a new path toward meaning. Whether the stories were literal truth or mythic truth hardly mattered. The Camino teaches you to recognise the difference—and the value of both. By the time I reached the stretch of woodland where the trees arch overhead like a cathedral, I felt the presence of all these layers of belief—the Christian, the mystical, the folk traditions, the whispers of Celtic Spain. They were not separate threads but a single tapestry, one that held its shape because of its contradictions, not despite them.

And amid that ancientness, I felt something shift inside me. For so long, I had walked as a man trying to *understand* his life, to piece together the meaning of heartbreak, loss, and the strange, irrevocable turning points that had shaped me. But here, as the path wound deeper into Galicia, I began walking not to understand my life—but to accept it. Acceptance is its own surrender. And surrender is its own kind of love.

With every footstep, I was reminded that I had not come to the Camino seeking salvation or answers. I had come for something quieter: to listen, to remember, to honour the man I had been and the man I was becoming. There was a moment— small, almost invisible—when I realised I was no longer striving to be healed. I was simply allowing myself to be human. And in that simple permission, the weight I had carried for so long began to loosen. Not vanish. Never vanish. But soften—enough for breath to return, enough for wonder to re-enter the body.

It was then I understood why I had returned to this road for a fourth time, be that more in my mind than the physical. The Camino is not a straight line; it is a spiral. Every return brings you closer to the centre of yourself. So it was that on the last descent toward Sarria, surrounded by the half-light of the Galician forests, I felt the presence of my grandfather again— the storyteller, the boundary rider, the voice that once set a young boy's heart alight. And I understood, with a clarity that startled me: Love had brought me here. Love had never stopped guiding me. And love—quiet, patient, unassuming— was still leading me on.

I recall with absolute clarity the final approach to Santiago—not only on my first pilgrimage along the French Route, but on the second as well. The steps I took on both journeys were as inward as they were outward. By then, many of my burdens had long been laid down: some at Cruz Ferro, some in whispered confessions to the wind, some simply surrendered to the rhythm of walking itself. With each kilometre, the weight on my back had lightened, but more importantly, the weight inside my chest had begun to loosen.

My mind's eye was sharper then—more present, more awake. Every sound, every footfall, every shifting shadow between the eucalyptus trunks seemed to carry its own message. The final stretch into Santiago is not just a road; it is a merging of realities—the physical present interwoven with the mythic past, the shadows and the light, the known and the unknown. It is a place where the old stories walk beside you.
On that path, I carried with me the haunting echo of my own **Santiago song**, the one that rose from the deepest part of me, summarising what the arrival meant: *coming home, not to a city but to a truth; not to a destination but to myself. Letting go of the past with a mindfulness of the present.*

The lyrics played in my mind like a quiet prayer. The words spoke of not looking back on the past—not because it did not matter, but because the Camino had already transformed it. The past had become a teacher, not a prison. The burdens, once sharp as broken glass, were now softened into memory, folded into the greater story of my life. Santiago was in my heart more than ever, and I understood it now with a certainty I never had before. Where once I had walked burdened by disbelief, wrestling with faith as though it were a rope burning between my hands, now I walked with a sense of clarity. My Christian upbringing—those early roots I had abandoned in adulthood—seemed not to return but to *transform*. The old stories did not demand belief; they illuminated understanding. And in that illumination, belief became something different from doctrine. It became recognised. Recognition of a Presence that had always walked beside me, even in the darkest nights. Recognition of love—quiet, persistent, unyielding. Recognition that destiny is not imposed but discovered.

And so, as the towers of Santiago's cathedral finally rose in the sunlight, I felt no surge of triumph or relief. Instead, there was a deep stillness—a knowing. I had walked farther than the miles suggested. I had descended deeper than the valleys I'd crossed. And I had risen higher than any mountain I had climbed.

Lavacolla, on the quiet outskirts of Santiago de Compostela, is for many pilgrims the last true stop on the French Way— and so it was for me on each of my Caminos. It felt like a threshold, a final exhale before the inward breath of arrival. By the time I reached it, my feet were tired, my heart was full, and the accumulated memories of the road seemed to gather around me like invisible companions.

The overnight stay there held a special warmth. The proprietor welcomed pilgrims with a hospitality that felt ancient— simple, sincere, unforced. The food was nourishing, the wine generous, the company unexpectedly intimate. I shared dinner with another lone pilgrim, each of us carrying our own story, each of us aware that we were on the cusp of something profound. It became a quiet flashback to my first Camino: the same sense of anticipation, the same humility before the unknown, the same feeling that every step was drawing me closer to a truth I could not yet articulate.

After we parted with the customary **"Buen Camino,"** I went to my room, weary but content. Before sleep claimed me, a small brochure caught my eye, and I found myself reading about the origin of the town's name. *Lavacolla*, it was explained, came from *lava*, meaning 'to wash'. For centuries, pilgrims had cleansed themselves in the stream here before entering Santiago—both for ritual purity and, quite practically, to spare the Cathedral from the stench of the great unwashed.

In medieval times, hygiene was a luxury, not a custom. To bathe before presenting oneself at the relics of St. James was not merely symbolic; it was merciful. And I could not help but smile at the thought that the famed *botafumeiro*—that massive incense-swinging thurible that arcs like a comet through the Cathedral transept—may have been introduced less as an expression of heavenly devotion and more as a device to fumigate the accumulated odour of thousands of weary pilgrims.

Even today, though times have changed and pilgrims are freshly showered and dressed in clean clothes, the botafumeiro remains the great spectacle of Santiago. Many a pilgrim, I suspect, attends the Pilgrim's Mass not out of devotion, but in hopes of witnessing those eight robed tiraboleiros heaving on the ropes, sending the great silver vessel soaring overhead like some celestial pendulum.

Still, behind the spectacle lies something ancient and true. Lavacolla marks the final purification—not of the body, but of the heart. A washing away of the last dust of the journey, before stepping into the sacred embrace of Santiago.

As I extinguished the light and lay back on the bed, I knew that in the morning I would walk the last kilometres with a quiet reverence. Not because of tradition, nor ritual, nor even the mass that awaited me—but because Lavacolla had reminded me that the Camino is as much about **letting go** as it is about arriving.

And I was ready now. Ready to enter not just a city, but a chapter of myself that had waited for years to be seen.

I rose in the pitch-black hours before dawn, long before even the whisper of morning light had stirred the sky. The albergue was still, the world unbreathing. I dressed quietly, laced my boots, and stepped out into the night where only my headlamp carved a thin blade of light through the darkness.

There is something ancient in that hour between night and dawn—something that belongs neither to the living nor the dead. In Galicia, a land steeped in myth and superstition, that feeling grows stronger. I had read of the old tales: the *meigas* —the witches—and their shadowy gatherings in the forest; the nocturnal cults that once wandered the hills with candles, seeking to lure weary pilgrims into darker paths before the sacred destination could redeem them.

Whether one believes such stories or not, they cling to the Iberian Peninsula like morning mist. And as I threaded my way through the trees, the crunch of gravel beneath my boots the only sound, I remembered a peculiar warning from a brochure: *If troubled by witches, draw a circle on the ground, step inside, and do not leave it until they pass.*

A strange piece of advice, yet the kind of superstition that endures for centuries because it once meant something to someone.

I did see lights flickering in the forest—tiny, uncertain glimmers, like fireflies or distant lanterns. For a moment, the old stories stirred in my imagination. *Was it witches? Meigas on their nocturnal wanderings?*

But no harm came. No circle was needed. On both my Caminos, superstition remained just that: a ghostly echo of a past that no longer had teeth. I pressed on.

Lavacolla faded behind me, and with each step I felt myself crossing into the final threshold of the Camino. The name itself—*lava*, to wash; *colla*, a hill—seemed fitting. Whether cleansing or climbing, the place had always prepared pilgrims for the last ascent of the spirit.

The path led me to **Monte do Gozo**—the Hill of Joy. Even in the dim blue dawn, I could just make out the distant spires of Santiago Cathedral. For medieval pilgrims, that first glimpse was said to reduce hardened men to tears. Even today, with roads and modernity pressing in on every side, the moment still held a certain power. I felt it in my chest, a rising warmth, a recognition: *I am nearly home.*

From there, the descent into Santiago was both physical and inner. Street by street, stone by stone, I walked with a growing solemnity until finally I stepped into the vast embrace of the **Praza do Obradoiro.**

The first time, it was emotional in a way I had never expected. My small band of brothers—those young companions who had walked with me through heat, storms, laughter, and exhaustion—were waiting for me. They welcomed me with open arms before we entered the Pilgrim's Mass together. There was a sense of belonging, of sharing a triumph that was larger than any one of us.

It felt like the culmination not only of my physical journey, but also of a deeper inner pilgrimage I had unknowingly begun long before I ever knew of the Camino.

The second time was different—subtler, quieter, almost solitary in its solemnity. There was no one waiting. No familiar faces. I entered the square alone, my boots echoing softly on the stone. This arrival was not triumphant; it was contemplative. And yet, in its quiet way, it felt more spiritual.

There was a gentle renewal in the solitude, a reminder that the Camino is not merely about companionship, but about the journey one must make inward, toward the self, toward truth, toward the soul's quiet unfolding.

I stood there with *sad eyes, perhaps*, but also with a heart rinsed clean by the long walk, the burdens released, the memories made sacred in their retelling.

Recall now, by the time I stepped onto the stones of the **Praza do Obradoiro,** I understood that I was not arriving at the end of a pilgrimage. I was arriving at the beginning of my true life. The burdens were behind me. The path ahead was open.

And the destiny I had sensed—faint, uncertain, trembling like a flame in the wind—now stood before me fully formed. I knew what I was meant for. I knew why the Camino had called me back. And for the first time in my life, I was walking toward the man I was always meant to be.

Santiago.

Walking along
singing my song
Heading for home
Santiago!

Starry eyes,
clear blue skies,
Heading for joy,
Santiago!

What's the point
in turning back where?
Look along the track there.
Walking to Santiago.

Travel far,
Calling for love
Cobblestone path,
Santiago!

Relieve pain
Put down your pack
You're almost home
Santiago!

What's the point
In turning back, where?
Look ahead along the track there.
Walking to Santiago.

Darkness gone
Tears of joy

Seeing the light.
Santiago!

Milky Way
Guiding my path
You're almost home.
Santiago!

What's the point
In turning back, where?
Look ahead along the track there.

Walking to Santiago!

Part 11: Homecoming.

I remember my vision of the entry into Santiago on each occasion of my Caminos. It was not for me, unlike I may have been for others. The morning silence, then the movement of the city as pilgrims take slow steps into Santiago; the city begins to unfold gently. I see fellow pilgrims as they walk along the narrow streets, feeling the cobblestones beneath their feet as the first light touches the buildings. The mist still lingers in the air, and the faint sound of a distant bell or a lone street sweeper is all they hear. And then, slowly, the silhouette of the cathedral rises in front of them, towering and radiant in the morning light. For me, it is a connection to my heart. Something I had not realised back then, a connection with the heart that I had not felt before.

I recall my final entry into the Cathedral. It was filled, as it always seemed to be during the Pilgrim's Mass. I remember standing there among the pilgrims I had walked beside, all of us waiting patiently for the celebration to begin—the pomp, the ceremony, the priests dressed in their finest vestments.

Yet amid all that splendour, I could not help thinking of the beggars at the cathedral doors—those who knelt outside, pleading for help from the church and from the pilgrims who passed by. Their presence lingered in my mind, even as the Mass unfolded.

My memory drifts back to the walk of a few blocks to receive my Compostela certificate, to have my pilgrim passport stamped as proof of the journey completed. I recall the moment in the Mass when the *botafumeiro* ceremony began— the great incense burner lifted by ropes, swung high above the congregation by eight monks. It soared from side to side across the cathedral, filling the air with smoke and awe.

As I did on all my Caminos, I wandered the streets of Santiago afterwards, alone. I sat at outdoor cafés, eating and drinking in a dazed state. I listened to the laughter and conversation of other pilgrims. I watched my own small band of brothers emerge from the shadows into the light of the street, one by one.

I remember climbing the steps up to the lower square behind the Cathedral: the **Quintana of the Dead**—once a burial ground until as late as 1780, now lined with small shops selling trinkets for travellers. Then another set of steps up into the **Quintana of the Living**, and in that place the shadows of pilgrims from centuries past seemed to move like gentle ghosts. But there was no fear. No witches to confront. No darkness to escape. For I had come out of the shadows by then, and into the light.

Finally, I climbed one more narrow staircase into a small room above a café, and there I fell into a deep, unbroken sleep—the kind only a pilgrim knows at the end of a very long journey.

On each of my Caminos, I stayed an extra day in Santiago and walked the streets alone. Pilgrims always greeted me I had met along The Way, sharing brief smiles, embraces, and fragments of stories before we drifted apart again. Those last wanderings felt like a gentle unwinding—a slow release from the long road behind me.

I always took the opportunity to visit the Cathedral again, to stand before the reported burial place of St James beneath the high altar. Following tradition, I descended the narrow stone stairs into the crypt. There, in the dim light, I knelt before the silver casket said to hold the bones of the apostle of Christ.

I had my doubts—serious doubts—that James ever came to Spain. But I prayed anyway, just in case I was wrong.

Then, like countless pilgrims before me, I climbed the steps behind the altar to embrace the golden statue of St James. I placed my arms around its shoulders, worn smooth by centuries of hands and hearts seeking connection, blessing, and closure. It was a gesture more symbolic than literal, yet deeply human. And yet—myth remains.

On each of my Caminos, I stayed on in Santiago for an extra day after arriving, wandering the streets alone in that strange, drifting mixture of exhaustion, fulfilment, and quiet disbelief. Pilgrims I had met along the Way would greet me with smiles or hugs, brief reunions of companionship forged in blisters, sweat, and miles. Yet, beneath the laughter of outdoor cafés and the warmth of shared meals with my small band of brothers, there was always a subtle ache—the knowledge that soon we would part, that these fleeting friendships would fade like mist in the morning sun. And they always did. For a while, we promised to keep in touch. For a while, we tried. But eventually the silence settled, and their absence felt like a kind of small death in my heart.

Still, my ritual remained. I would visit the Cathedral again, not as a triumphant pilgrim entering for the first time, but as a man trying to understand what he had walked for. I made my way down into the crypt where the reported remains of St. James rest beneath the altar. I always knelt, though I held doubts—grave doubts—about whether the apostle had ever set foot on Spanish soil. History records he was beheaded in Jerusalem in

40 AD by King Herod Agrippa. Legends claim his body, Viking-style, drifted by miraculous barge to the Iberian Peninsula. That his disciples buried him, that for eight hundred years his resting place was forgotten until a fisherman's vision brought it to light. That the bones were blessed, enshrined, and displayed strategically to stir faith and funding for wars against the Moors. That St. James would later appear in battle on a white steed leading troops into battle is pure myth, but pilgrims still return to revisit his remains, perhaps in homage to the saint, perhaps in humble resignation to their own mystery and myth of a life.

Every Camino ended the same way for me: not with triumph or revelation, but with a quiet, unsettling feeling that the journey was not yet complete. Maybe that's why I kept coming back—three Caminos, each different but the same in essence.

The road kept calling me back, not because I had walked the streets of Santiago slowly letting the city reveal itself in small fragments: a pilgrim limping toward the Cathedral; a shopkeeper sweeping the stone steps; the smell of fresh bread drifting from a bakery tucked between two narrow walls. And then, always, the faces—pilgrims of every age, every story, every wound. Some wore the glow of victory. Others carried the weariness of battle. A few looked as though they had come seeking salvation and found only more questions. I knew that feeling well.

For all my miles, for all the dust on my boots, I was still wrestling with the same familiar struggle: how to surrender the self completely. How to let go of the world's distractions, its pleasures, its illusions. How to give myself entirely to the God of my understanding when my heart constantly wandered. I had often walked with my body on the Camino. Still, my soul tugged toward earthly desires—most often toward the beauty of a woman, the longing for companionship, the craving for affection that felt more immediate than the silent call of God.

I always stayed an extra day in Santiago, walked the streets slowly in the morning, letting the city reveal itself in small fragments: a pilgrim limping toward the Cathedral; a shopkeeper sweeping the stone steps; the smell of fresh bread drifting from a bakery tucked between two narrow walls. And then, always, the faces—pilgrims of every age, every story, every wound. Some wore the glow of victory. Others carried the weariness of battle. A few looked as though they had come seeking salvation and found only more questions. I knew that feeling well.

For all my miles, for all the dust on my boots, I was still wrestling with the same familiar struggle: how to surrender the self completely. How to let go of the world's distractions, its pleasures, its illusions. How to give myself entirely to the God of my understanding when my heart constantly wandered. I had often walked with my body on the Camino. Still, my soul tugged toward earthly desires—most often toward the beauty of a woman, the longing for companionship, the craving for affection that felt more immediate than the silent call of God. It was a battle I rarely spoke of, but one that shaped every step of my pilgrimages. The Camino exposes you. It strips you down, and not because I had learnt all its. Only in hindsight—often years later—do you understand what it was trying to teach you.

Looking back now, I see clearly what I could not see on my first, or even my second and third Camino: that I was not walking toward a destination, but away from myself. Away from the man who tried to fit into the world like a square peg in a round hole. Away from the pain, the grief, the tragedies that had carved hollows inside me. Away from the memories I wasn't ready to face.

Santiago had always meant "arrival," but each time I stood in the plaza before the Cathedral, I felt more like a man at the beginning of something rather than at the end. The square would fill with rejoicing pilgrims, cheering, crying, and taking photos. Meanwhile, I often stood a little apart, feeling both inside and outside of their joy. Not lonely—just aware that my Camino was never about celebration. It was about revelation. And sometimes revelation arrives slowly, painfully, like dawn through a cloudy sky.

As I wandered through the old town that day, I thought about my first Camino—the naïve hope, the raw innocence, the eagerness to be transformed. And I thought about my second, where the road no longer surprised me but still shaped me, reshaped me, and refused to let me hide from myself.

There were moments along those roads—small, easily missed moments—that only now return with clarity. The older man sitting alone on a stone wall, who nodded at me with a knowing I didn't understand then. The girl in the albergue who cried quietly into her hands, thinking no one noticed. The priest who told me, "Transformation is not an event, but a slow surrender." The storm that pinned me down in the Meseta forced me to sit still with my thoughts. The way the sun rose one morning was like a whispered promise that I was not walking alone, even when I felt I was.

I had missed so much in the moment. But memory is patient—it gives you back what you weren't ready to receive.

And so I walked again that morning in Santiago, feeling the weight of my Caminos settle differently now—not as unfinished stories, but as mirrors. Mirrors reflecting who I had been, and perhaps who I was meant to become.

When midday approached, I made my way back toward the Cathedral plaza. Pilgrims were gathering again for the Mass, filling the air with a mixture of excitement, exhaustion, and reverence. I watched them, knowing that each carried a private battle, a private hope, a private transformation unfolding in its own time. And as I stood there, in the sunlight of the square, I realised something simple yet profound: The Camino doesn't end in Santiago. It never has. It continues in every choice, every surrender, every moment of honesty that follows.

For the first time in years, I felt a quiet shift inside me—not a revelation, but a soft opening, like a door I had not noticed before. A whisper without words. An invitation to stop walking away from myself and begin walking toward something deeper. The journey, it seemed, was only beginning.

I hadn't realised it then—on my earlier Caminos, or even in the years that followed—but I see it clearly now: the "good life" I had lived in a first-world sense was slowly drifting away, like the tide slipping back from the shore. And just as surely as the tide returns, it always comes back different, reshaping the sand beneath it. Nature repeats itself, yes, but never in the same way. Each moment is a beginning born of an ending.

It was in this spirit of reflection that I wandered the familiar streets of Santiago at the end of yet another Camino, carrying the strange mixture of fatigue, gratitude, sadness, and longing that always visited me in those final hours. I moved almost by instinct, following a path I had taken on every pilgrimage, until I found myself—as locals so often do—walking toward the quiet sanctuary of **Alameda Park**, not ten minutes from the Cathedral.

In many ways, that park rivals the Cathedral itself. A sanctuary of a different order. A cathedral made of trees and air and memory. There are lush gardens, stone monuments worn by time, and the grand tiered steps that descend like an invitation to slow down. And tucked among all of this is an unassuming stone bench that, to the unknowing eye, means nothing. But to those who understand, it holds thousands of secrets.

Passionate Revelations.

Banco Acústico. *The Bench of Whispers.* Some call it the *Lovers' Bench.* Its shape is semicircular, designed so that if you gently rest your head against the stone back and whisper, your voice echoes louder at the far end than when it left your lips—an intimate trick of acoustics, like the whispering galleries in St. Paul's or Grand Central Station. The bench was placed there in 1916 and became a refuge for young lovers during the long era of moral strictures of the Franco regime, when public affection was forbidden. But a walk in the park was innocent. And a whispered word—carried along the arc of stone to a waiting heart—was its own quiet rebellion.

I remember the first time I sat there, eucalyptus trees standing like silent guardians around me. Their scent caught me off-guard—clean, sharp, familiar. It smelled like home as though Australia had reached across oceans to tap me gently on the shoulder.

I sat there often, the stone cool against my back, listening to the strange intimacy of sound, feeling the soft sway of branches overhead. I thought of another seeker, a long way from Santiago: Siddhartha beneath the Bodhi tree, stepping beyond doctrine into enlightenment. He, too, had questioned the accepted truths of his world. He, too, had gone searching for something beyond the surface of things.
And as I sat under the eucalyptus, in the stillness of the park, I realised that my own spiritual journey—my multiple Caminos, my wandering mind, my craving for love, my longing for God—was born of the same impulse. Not rebellion, not escape, but

the need to know. To step beyond the inherited stories and find the truth that whispers beneath them.

There, on the Bench of Whispers, with nothing but memory and the faint rustle of leaves for company, I felt again the subtle stirring that had followed me through all my Caminos:

A question I had never fully formed. An answer I had never fully received. A presence I could never quite touch, yet never escape. And I knew—more than ever—that the Camino had not ended in Santiago. The Camino never ends.

So, in my search for surrender to the Way, I had yet to understand what surrender truly meant. I thought it was an act of letting go, a quiet bowing of the head, a willingness to release the past. But surrender—real surrender—asks far more. It asks for the unravelling of the self, the dissolution of illusions, the courage to see what lies beneath the surface of one's desires. I did not know this then. But I know it now.

Women had walked into my life along the Camino with a spiritual precision. Some stayed a day, some an hour, some only long enough to leave a trace—a smile, a conversation, a fleeting warmth that lingered long after they were gone. They were not simply companions along the road; they were mirrors, revealing corners of my heart I was not ready to face. They showed me my need for connection, my vulnerability, my loneliness, my longing to be held, understood, desired. I found myself believing that the touch of a woman could answer the ache within me, or at least quiet it for a while. I mistook affection for salvation, intimacy for healing, flesh for spirit. It was not intentional—it was human. But the result was always the same: a momentary warmth followed by an echoing emptiness. A sweetness that inevitably turned into sadness when the road bent and she walked one way while I walked another. It took me years on Caminos, in fact, to recognise the pattern. To see that what I had been seeking in women was not romance. It was God. Or rather, the sense of divine presence I believed I had lost.

The attraction, the distraction, the longing—they were signs of a deeper hunger, a spiritual thirst I kept trying to quench with human touch. And though each encounter brought beauty and tenderness, it also brought pain, because it was never meant to fill the hollow that only surrender could reach.

And so the Camino called me back again and again. Not for the landscapes. Not for the fellowship. Not even for the healing of grief, though that too played its part. I returned because each pilgrimage revealed another layer of myself I had refused to see. Because the road had a way of stripping me bare—of exposing the beliefs I clung to, the illusions I hid behind, the patterns I repeated without understanding why. And because somewhere deep inside, I knew that surrender was not a single act but a lifelong unfolding. Every Camino was an attempt to let go. Every Camino failed, because I wasn't ready. Every Camino succeeded, because it showed me the next piece of the truth. I returned because I was still learning. I returned because something sacred was still calling. I returned because the Way was not finished with me. And perhaps—just perhaps—I returned because I was not finished with myself.

I seemed, in many respects, to be looking back on my former life through the lens of the world's standards. By those measures, I had lived a good life—comfortable, educated, secure. And yet, without any clear warning signs, the ground beneath that life began to shift. On shifting sands, the life that once defined me slowly started to dissolve. Only on reflection did the Camino reveal this quiet erosion. Only then did I see how necessary it was.

The Way was preparing me long before I understood for what. Each step, each silence, each moment of fatigue was nudging me toward an awakening—a stripping away of illusions so that truth could find room to speak.

The tides of life would come and go, carrying me forward as they always had, but it took more than one Camino for me to recognise that the direction of real greatness is not outward at all. The true pilgrimage is inward.

Looking back now, I see that my pilgrimages were training me for a deeper journey, one far more demanding than the physical road through Spain. Even my writings—novels, songs, stories of fiction and truth—were part of that preparation. At the time, I believed they were messages for others, but upon reflection, I see they were speaking first and foremost to me. The Camino had been whispering all along. I sought spiritual healing in human arms, divine presence in another's smile. It was not wrong; it was simply incomplete. With each encounter came tenderness—and pain. A sweetness followed by the sting of departure, reminding me always that the refuge I sought could not be found outside myself.

The Way strips you down. It allows nothing unnecessary to survive. Somewhere between the villages and vineyards, between the storms and sunrises, I began to see my striving for what it was: a cycle of grasping and losing, gaining and returning, like the tide repeating itself across the sand.

Coming home from my first Camino left me on a deceptive path—one paved not with wisdom but with illusions. I mistook the afterglow of the pilgrimage for a mandate to *do*, to *chase*, to *achieve*. I pursued ideas as if each new project carried the pot of gold at the end of some worldly rainbow. But the harder I chased, the further away that rainbow fled. What I did not yet understand was that the Camino had not ended. I had only walked its physical length. The inward path —the one that required surrender, honesty, and stillness—had barely begun.

My ambition, fevered and misguided, carried me to the point of collapse. Exhaustion forced me into rehabilitation—an enforced stillness. And only then, stripped of pretence, did I see the truth clearly: The world I was striving for was not my destination. It was only the shadow of a deeper calling.

The outward achievements I thought mattered were merely symbols of something that lived within me, something I could not yet name. I had tasted the elixir of life on the Camino, but its meaning had not yet ripened. My soul, it seemed, was still on pilgrimage. So I went searching again, not across oceans this time, but within.

I chose a quiet place—a hilltop overlooking the wild coastline of Long Reef. The dawn broke beautifully, and the colours of the sky brought back memories of those early Camino mornings. I chose when the world felt suspended between night and blessing.

I descended the pathway to the beach, letting the crash of the waves drown out the noisy questions in my mind. The sound was like Finisterre—the literal "end of the earth"—where pilgrims walk when they are not yet finished with their journey, when they need the Atlantic to speak to them. My feet waded into the cold water. A glimmer caught my eye: sunlight reflecting off something riding the wave. A piece of driftwood, skimming toward the shore as though sent. I walked into the swell and retrieved it. A rough piece of wood—weathered, battered, stripped bare of whatever purpose it once held. But it was beautiful. The grain… the depth of colour. Mahogany.

So things stirred in me.

I remembered the story of the **Mahogany Ship**—that mysterious Portuguese or Spanish caravel half-buried in the dunes of Victoria—a ghost from the Age of Discovery. No one knew how it got there. Some believed it was one of the early spice ships—part of that fierce, centuries-long war over cloves, cinnamon, nutmeg… commodities worth more than gold. Ships made for perilous journeys across the Indian Ocean, around Africa, or through uncharted waters between Indonesia and India.

Standing there with that driftwood in my hands, I wondered: *Could this piece be from something like that? A remnant of the forgotten world of caravels? Or just a humble scrap the sea had chosen to deliver to me now, at this very moment?* Either way, it felt like a sign.

That driftwood lit a spark of intrigue in me, and soon research consumed my thoughts—studies of caravels, spice routes, lost ships, disappeared fleets. Were there still clues hidden somewhere? Could Portugal hold answers?

That became my **first reason** for another Camino: to learn what I could about the age of **caravels** and the ships that vanished into history.

Then came the **second reason** just as quickly. The route from Lisbon passed not far from **Fátima**, the site of the 1917 apparition of the Virgin Mary—a place steeped in mystery, controversy, devotion. Having visited Lourdes, I felt compelled to witness this other axis of Marian pilgrimage. And then, almost inexplicably, a **third reason** presented itself: a message from **a Portuguese woman** on Facebook. This unexpected beauty reached out when I announced my intention to walk the Portuguese Camino. A thread of curiosity tugged at me. Maybe destiny tugged too. Three quests. Three apparent purposes. All external.All shimmering like lures.

Only later would I understand that these too were false flags— beautiful illusions that pointed me outward when the true Camino still waited within. But in my haste, I prepared myself for another quest. Another road. Another search. And so, the next stage of my quest, another Camino pilgrim life began.

I had a new goal—or so I believed. A host of butterfly-brain flashes stirred through my mind, each one brighter than the last. The Portuguese Way of the Camino, the mystery of the mahogany caravel wreck discovered off our Australian coastline a century and a half ago… it all seemed woven together by threads of desire. I had researched the secrets of the Templars, their shadowy link to the early spice caravels, their fortresses standing like silent guardians not far from the Portuguese route. Perhaps, I thought, they held the answers. Perhaps their forgotten manuscripts or hidden chambers preserved the key to the Mahogany Ship enigma. Their story alone gave me yet more enthusiasm for the journey.

And then there was **Fátima**—just a stone's throw from the Camino path—the site of the apparitions of the Virgin Mary toward the end of the First World War. The three secrets given to the shepherd children. The first two had already come to pass—the second being the horror of the Second World War. But the third… the third was the most frightening of all. The eldest child had written it down in a sealed letter to the Pope, meant to be revealed in the early 1960s. But upon reading it, the Pope deemed it too terrible for humanity to know. Now it lies locked away in a vault deep within the Vatican.

And looking at the world as it unfolds today—its upheavals, divisions, the trembling of old institutions—I could not help but feel that the unreleased prophecy had begun to seep into present reality. Scenes from the Book of Revelation, the predictions of Nostradamus, the warnings of ancient mystics… all seemed to echo through our age.
I shook off those feelings—the visions of horror that flickered in my imagination—and turned instead to thoughts of the beauty that awaited me in Portugal. I had already visualised a tender relationship, a romance that felt destined. The Portuguese beauty who had contacted me on Facebook after I announced my intentions to walk the Camino… in my haste, I had allowed my imagination to spin a story of hope and companionship. Looking back now, I see that this too belonged to the realm of dreams—a wild spark that burned brightly but brought no lasting good to either of us.

Yet at the time, I felt propelled by not one, but three goals. Three quests like banners raised before me, each one giving me reason to prepare myself for a new adventure.

So I made up my mind. I would start my Camino in **Lisbon.** I would visit museums and archives, search for old shipping records, and seek any remaining fragments of Templar lore. I would walk among the castles and battlements where knights once guarded medieval pilgrims.

I would follow the ancient Portuguese traditions of faith and mystery. I would try to understand whether the **Mahogany Ship** truly belonged to the old spice fleets that sailed between India and Indonesia. And, perhaps, I would find meaning in Fátima's message—or in the company of someone new. But the Camino had other lessons in store for me.

What unfolded was a long, winding journey—one that drew me away from the world's external quests, its glittering lures and seductive mysteries. And slowly, step by step, it brought me back to the contemplative truth of pilgrimage itself. In the end, the real Camino was not in the Templars, the ships, the prophecies, or the dreams of romance.
It was in the letting go. The slow shedding of illusions until only the inner path remained.

I convinced myself I had a destiny to uncover: the truth of the mahogany caravel believed to have washed up on our distant Australian shores long before any official explorer laid claim. A silent witness from the Age of Discovery, from the spice routes and the intrigue of empires. Mahogany — the very same timber that now appeared at my feet on the sands at Long Reef, as if carried from another world, another time, another purpose. That driftwood, whether coincidence or providence, rekindled an old restlessness. I had once written of hidden treasure beneath the surface of things — of how a pilgrim does not always seek gold, but the knowledge that lies behind gold, and the longing behind knowledge. Now, years later, I found myself chasing yet another outward symbol of an inward truth I still had not fully recognised. In those days, before the clarity that would come later, I imagined myself a seeker of lost caravels, Templar secrets, and forgotten histories. That the very earth of Portugal might whisper to me what the sands of Victoria had concealed. The Templars — guardians of pilgrims, keepers of mysteries, silhouettes standing between the known world and the divine — beckoned me with their stone fortresses and ancient routes.

Fantasy to Reality.

I traced their lines on the map of Portugal as if they might point me towards something that had been ordained for me alone.

I was a pilgrim chasing signs, not yet ready to accept the one truth every true pilgrim eventually learns: The treasure of the Camino is not found by discovering something new —but by rediscovering what had always been yours. I had walked thousands of kilometres through Spain, over mountains, across plains, among pilgrims from every corner of the earth. I had wept at the cathedral steps and stood before the relics of the Apostle, feeling the old faith rise in me, a feeling my modern mind had long resisted. And still I had not understood.

Now, preparing for the Portuguese Way, I thought my destiny lay in uncovering shipwrecks and Templar codes. I clung to the outward, unaware that something far more intimate was being prepared in the quiet spaces of my soul.

I set out for **Portugal** believing I had three reasons for the journey. But the Camino, in its divine patience, had only one reason for me: Each step would bring me closer not to the caravel, nor to the secrets of Fatima, nor to the imagined romance of a distant woman — but to the contemplative, surrendered life that had been calling me since the first day I set foot on the Way. A pilgrim does not choose the treasure; the treasure chooses the pilgrim. And so, with my pack on my shoulders and my mind swirling with goals, dreams, and illusions, I walked toward Portugal unaware the Camino was preparing to teach me the last great lesson — the one I had run from even as I sought it: That every outward journey is only a mirror of the journey within.

Lisbon greeted me not as a city but as an echo — a place where centuries seem to linger in the air, where the stones themselves hold memory. Stepping into the old quarters, I felt as though I were walking into a dream that had been waiting for my arrival.

The early morning light washed over the white facades, and trams clattered over rails like relics of another age, refusing to disappear. I stood on the high ground above the Tagus River, imagining the caravels that once set sail from these very waters — carrying spices, secrets, and the restless hopes of nations. It struck me then that those ancient ships had something in common with pilgrims: both set out into the unknown not to escape, but to discover.

My distraction — if I am honest — came not from shipwreck mysteries nor Templar legends, but from the sudden arrival of a woman who seemed to walk straight out of some half-forgotten dream. My Facebook connection — she was Portuguese, striking in that effortless way that Lisbon women can be — a mix of elegance, self-possession, and something ancient in the eyes. A doctor, she said, though that alone didn't capture her. She carried herself like someone accustomed to thinking deeply about the world, a philosopher of Portuguese history no less, with a love of stories carved into the stones of her own country.

But truth be told, as she spoke of kings, caravels, and crusading orders, my mind wandered. I was not listening to history. I was listening to her voice.

There was a moment — I remember it clearly — when the afternoon sunlight caught her hair, and she turned to point out an old Manueline doorway. In that pause, in that soft glow of Lisbon's light, I felt an almost adolescent jolt inside me—a desire not of romance, nor companionship, but of fire. I wanted to take her in my arms. I wanted to feel life burning again — the kind of passion that sweeps through a man who has lived too long in shadows. But I brushed it aside, as politely as one brushes away a passing thought. I had come for other reasons. Or so I told myself.

She guided me through the tangle of Lisbon's narrow streets, effortlessly weaving history into the walk — how the great earthquake reshaped the city; how pilgrims once moved through Alfama; how sailors, saints, and sinners had all touched these stones. I nodded, half-listening, half adrift in the scent of her perfume. Soon we found ourselves sitting at a small outdoor café in Baixa, the kind with white tablecloths and the faint sound of fado drifting through open windows. We shared a simple lunch — some grilled fish, olives, and a light Vinho Verde. She spoke about the Portuguese Way as if it were an old friend. I wanted to tell her what was happening inside me. I didn't. The Camino had a way of testing one's silence.

After lunch, with the effortless authority of someone who knows the city's pulse, she directed me toward the Cathedral. "You must get your pilgrim passport," she said.
"Without it, you are only a tourist. With it, you are a pilgrim again."
She said "pilgrim" as if it meant something sacred. remember watching her walk away, her figure shrinking into the flow of

Lisbon life. Part of me wanted to run after her. Another part — the pilgrim part — knew that Camino encounters are like sparks: brief, illuminating, and not meant to be grasped.

And so I turned toward the Sé Cathedral, carrying in me both the weight of desire and the whisper of destiny. The passport I would receive there was more than a document — it would become the quiet witness to what the Camino was preparing to reveal. But at that moment, I was still just a man in Lisbon, torn between two roads: one of passion, and one of pilgrimage. Little did I know how they would soon intertwine.

I made my way to the **Sé Cathedral in Alfama,** the traditional starting point for the Portuguese Way. I purchased my Camino passport, a necessity to get discounted accommodation along the way. Still, with each stay at an albergue, I received a stamp as proof of my journey, ensuring the reward of a Compostela certificate at the end of The Way. The Church, I noticed a heavy Romanesque structure, solemn in posture, as though guarding the centuries of prayer embedded in its walls. I entered quietly, letting the dim light settle around me. The air smelled faintly of wax and stone. The atmosphere was my beginning — as the cathedral had been the beginning for countless others. But as I stood before the altar, I sensed that, unlike before, I was not asking for strength or guidance. Instead, I stood there silently, unsure what to ask at all. The Camino had already begun to strip away my outward quests.

The departure from **Lisbon** came with a strange mixture of anticipation and reluctance. She insisted on driving me to the outer boundary of the city, as if wanting to escort me not merely to the Camino's beginning but to the threshold of whatever destiny was unfolding. The morning light shimmered on the Tagus, and the pulse of Lisbon thinned as we left the old neighbourhoods behind.

We stopped at what John Brierley's guidebook indicated as the entry point to the Camino path — a modest turnout beside the roadway, a lane marked with a yellow arrow fading under years of weather. I stood there awkwardly with my pack, feeling both like a pilgrim and like a man about to lose something precious. She stepped close. For a moment, neither of us spoke. Then she kissed me — not the polite farewell kiss of acquaintances, but something deeper, hungry, certain. A kiss that said *we could have been something* if life were arranged differently. It lingered, grew, and became almost reckless.

We broke apart only when a truck roared past, the driver leaning on his horn as if blessing or cursing our embrace. Perhaps it was a divine joke, perhaps a warning, or perhaps simply a Portuguese truck driver with strong opinions about roadside passion. She laughed and touched my cheek. And then — she was gone. Her car dwindled into the distance while I stood with Brierley's guide open in my hands. His sacred arrows were meant to point the way. But the very first one betrayed me. The path he described, God rest his soul, no longer existed. Urban growth had swallowed it, rerouted it, changed the shape of the pilgrim's first steps. I walked back and forth searching for a marker, a sign, a hint of yellow paint. Nothing. I was forced to take a detour — across unfamiliar streets, through industrial zones, guessing my way like a blind man following instinct alone. And always, behind my confusion, the lingering pull of the Portuguese woman.

I found myself replaying the kiss, the density of her presence, the way her voice had shaped Lisbon's history into living colour. My heart tugged toward her, but my feet — stubborn as they were — moved forward. I reminded myself she would join me in Porto in a few days, travelling by train. That thought softened the ache of departure. But it also clouded the clarity of the pilgrimage.

As the day lengthened and the detour grew stranger, I felt the first cracks in the illusions I carried. The Camino was already reminding me — gently — that I had brought too many external quests, too many desires, too many stories not my own. The mysteries of the Grail, the Templars, the Caravels, the Mahogany Ship — all swirled inside me, a pilgrim with a scholar's burden. Yet the detour forced me into a more primal mindset: *Where will I eat? Where will I sleep? Will there be a bed at the end of this day?*

I let go of grand theories and settled into the simple rhythm of a pilgrim's first fears. Somewhere along that unfamiliar road, I remembered Brierley's footnote — the verse tucked away at the end of his foreword. I stopped under the shade of an olive tree and read it: "If you find nothing new, you will simply end up with an apartment in the City of Death. If you make love with the Divine now, in the next life you will have the face of satisfied desire. So plunge into the truth; find out who the Teacher is. Believe in the Great Sound."

The words landed like a quiet bell in the chest. I closed the guidebook and took a deep breath. The woman was behind me. The road was before me. And somewhere between the two stood the person I was becoming. With that, I tightened my pack, stepped back onto the road, and let the Camino — once again — reclaim my wandering heart.

It had taken me until now to realise this as I recall those moments, my tramp through night between crops, mindful of the dangers of stepping on a sleeping serpent of the night, but relieved at last to arrive at another village and being given refuge by a kindly priest to sleep in the newly built gymnasium, I settled down to sleep on a volting horse as my bed for the night, for I was on a mission—though not one sanctioned by any authority, nor mapped by any guidebook. It was a mission stitched together by the whims of chance, by the roadless stretches where even the dust seemed uncertain of its direction, by the dying embers of a day that offered neither mercy nor meaning. I had become dependent on whatever the Camino allowed: the uneven rhythms of my feet on gravel, the distant bark of a farm dog, the occasional shade thrown by a solitary tree as if offering sanctuary to a weary traveller who had forgotten what sanctuary meant. Hunger gnawed at me; thirst clung to my throat like a silent accusation. I pressed on regardless, pulled forward by something older than intention, older even than the pilgrimage itself.

Late in the evening, I arrived at a small village—if one could call it that—little more than a scatter of stone houses hunched together against the wind. No shops, no open bars, no fountain offering relief. Just silence. The kind of silence that tests a pilgrim's resolve. Then, as if placed there by divine mischief, I saw a small light trembling at the end of a dirt track between two fields of crops. A café? A house? A refuge? I couldn't know, but I followed it because that is what a pilgrim does: he follows the faintest flicker when everything else has gone dark.

Inside, an older woman greeted me without a word—only eyes that recognised the look of a man who carried more emptiness inside him than he showed on the outside. She didn't understand English, and I understood nothing of her dialect, yet the hunger and thirst on my face spoke a language older than words. She prepared a small sandwich, humble but perfect, and placed it in my hands as though offering a sacrament.

Outside, farm workers sat in the warm night air drinking beer, their skin bronzed and lined, their expressions fixed on a small television balanced haphazardly on a crate. On the screen, a heroic Spanish female matador danced with death in the arena, her cape swirling like a blood-red comet. The bull charged, massive and magnificent, and she turned with a grace that defied logic.

"¡Olé!" they cried aloud, every time she completed a pass— men who had spent their lives coaxing miracles from stubborn earth now entranced by her mastery over the raw, pulsing force before her.

I ate the older woman's sandwich slowly, each bite awakening something in me I had not realised had fallen asleep.

Gratitude, perhaps. Or humility. Or that quiet sense that life, even when stripped of comfort and certainty, still finds a way to offer small mercies—if we are willing to see them.

The workers kept shouting "¡Olé!" at the screen, their voices rising and falling with the rhythm of the matador's dance. As I watched her—a lone figure standing boldly before the bull—I felt something shift inside me. She moved with a courage I envied, a sureness of purpose I had long abandoned. She did not hesitate. She did not shrink. She did not question her place in the arena.

I, on the other hand, had lived much of my life trying to be what others needed, what society expected, what circumstance demanded. A square peg fitting its edges to fit into a round hole. On the Camino, I had begun sanding away the old shape, but it was slow and painful work.

When the matador delivered the final pass, poised and unflinching, the workers erupted in cheers. I found myself clapping too—not for the bullfight, but for the reminder that there are moments in life when you must stand your ground, even when everything charges at you with horns lowered.

The older woman pointed the Way to the next village, for in her kindness, she had phoned the priest to secure me a place to rest my head. It was but a two-kilometre walk in pitch-black darkness. I thanked her with a pilgrim's sincerity—awkward, fumbling, heartfelt.

In the gymnasium I recalled, the air was warm with the breath of night's silence. I lay there listening to the murmur of night animals, the distant cry of an owl, the whisper of wind through the gaps in the stillness. It was then, staring at the rafters, that I understood something I had resisted for years. The Camino wasn't teaching me how to escape my former life; it was teaching me how to surrender to the life I had been avoiding all along. Not the life measured by careers, possessions, or achievements. Not the life arranged around pleasing others or meeting expectations. But the life that emerges when there is nothing left to hold on to but truth. The truth of who you are—the truth of what you desire.

The truth of what breaks you. And the truth of what heals you. I eventually fell asleep, though I don't recall exactly when. The body gives out after enough miles, enough hunger, enough revelations. But as I drifted off, I thought of the Portuguese woman—her intellect sharp as a blade, her presence unsettlingly magnetic. I thought of how easily desire can rise on the Camino, as if each step strips away a layer of resistance, leaving you raw, vulnerable, exposed. I thought of the bullfighter, facing her fear with elegance. And the older woman, giving generously from her little. And the workers, finding joy in the heat of a long day's end.

And I realised that every one of them had become part of my pilgrimage, whether they knew it or not. The Camino is never walked alone. Even when you think you are.

Inner Resurrection.

Dawn seeped slowly into the gymnasium, a diluted grey light filtering through the skylight window. I woke stiff, the taste of dust in my mouth, and for a few disoriented seconds, I didn't remember where I was. Then the sound of the wind outside shifting brought it all back—the detour, the exhaustion, the matador, the older woman, and the strange sense of having crossed some invisible threshold during the night.

As I stepped back onto the roadway, the cool air on my face, I found my thoughts drifting again to the Portuguese woman. Although I had dreamed of a relationship with a foreign beauty, she had arrived in my life unexpectedly in Lisbon, as the Camino often arranges these things—without warning, without logic, without any regard for the plans you think you have. Her presence had unsettled me from the start. Not because of anything she did, but because she represented something I had long kept buried: the possibility of desire after devastation, of intimacy after loss, of life after long seasons of quiet despair.

On the first Camino, I would not have recognised this sensation. I walked then with the innocence of someone who thought the Camino was merely a long-distance trail with historical charm and spiritual undertones. I thought I was walking *to* something. On the second Camino, I walked like a man trying to outrun himself. The grief, the unanswered questions, the cracks in the façade of a once "stable life" were all there, but I did not yet dare to face them. I walked with weight—physical, emotional, invisible. But this third Camino was different. It was as if the first two had whispered truths I could not yet hear. And only now—years later, with life having shattered and reformed me—did those whispers rise into full voice.

This time, the Camino was not a path beneath my feet. It was a mirror. And the Portuguese woman was part of that reflection. She awakened in me the very desires I had suppressed: to belong, to be held, to feel alive in a way that neither achievement nor endurance nor stoic suffering could offer. As I walked through the quiet morning, fields stretching wide and golden on either side, I realised this uncomfortable truth: She represented the life I thought I had lost the right to feel again. Desire not dulled by tragedy. Connection not sabotaged by fear. Tenderness not shadowed by guilt.

I remembered the way she had kissed me on the boundary of Lisbon—her hand on my cheek, the warmth of her breath, the lingering imprint of her lips. And yet, even as my body remembered, another part of me knew that she was not the destination. She was the signpost. A marker pointing to the deeper work the Camino was now demanding of me. Surrender. Not the passive surrender of giving up—something I had tasted too often in the darker nights of my life—but the surrender of opening. Opening to the unknown. To vulnerability. To the truth I had been avoiding since my first pilgrimage.

I walked on, the gravel crunching beneath my boots, and thought about how many times I had mistaken endurance for transformation. How many times had I pushed forward, thinking that mileage equalled meaning? But transformation requires more than miles. It requires honesty. It requires stripping away the memories. It was asking me to walk deeper.

It requires surrendering to the life waiting beneath the life we cling to. By the time I stopped for water at a roadside fountain, I felt a strange clarity settling over me. This third Camino was not asking me to walk further, Deeper into myself. Deeper into the wounds I had refused to face. Deeper into the desires I had silenced. Deeper into the truth that pilgrimage is not a journey with an endpoint—it is a perpetual unravelling.

And somehow, in ways I couldn't yet explain, the Portuguese woman had become part of that unravelling. Not because of romance, or longing, or the fantasy of what might come next —but because she stirred awake a part of me that had been dormant since long before I first set foot on the Camino.

A part of me that wanted to live again.

Being lost in a delusion can make me feel comforted for a time, but the fog must lift eventually, as it always does. Somewhere in the black of my mind, I heard a voice: " Trust in the slow work of God." I discouraged that thought, shouldered my pack, tightened the straps, and kept walking. I knew she would meet me in **Porto** in a few days, just as she had promised. But I also knew that the real meeting was not between her and me. It was between the man I was becoming and me.

Oh! I've tramped the byways.
From St. Jean on the Way
Followed my star
On the Santiago Way.

Couldn't find love there
So I tramped a new route
Trudging the pathway

From old Lisbon Town.

Just another Jesus
On the road again
Looking for Mary Magdalene,
Looking for Madgdalen.

Apple trees are plenty.
You can pick your fill.
Tomatoes are free
To eat by the bushel

Wild berries grow
On this side of The Way
Taste the bittersweet
Of this lonely byway.

Peaches for the taking
Plums picked for free
Grapes for your fill
Cain sugar for your tea.
So many windows
That never shed light
Dark eyes on The Way
Ladies of the night.

She's calling me now.
Some girl of my dreams
Just another sad song
In Lisbon.

Maybe she's in Paris.
Could it be London Town?
Here on this pathway

A handful of sand.

Memories of the past
Just fading away
Is it just another sad song
In Lisbon.

Looking for Mary Magdalene
Looking for Magdalene.

Birds are flying free,
over there in Havama.
Flowers are blooming'
Somewhere in Oceania.

Is this my crown of thorns
A memory stone on The Way
Or just another sad song
In Lisbon.

The memory of the Tejo plains still clung to me as I approached the outskirts of **Porto**—a collage of colours, sensations, and half-formed meanings that seemed to rise and dissolve like mist each time I tried to grasp them.

Those early days along the Portuguese way had blurred into one long ribbon of orchards and riverbanks, Templar stories murmured by older men in village squares, and the rhythmic percussion of my poles tapping out the heartbeat of a pilgrim determined to uncover some long-buried truth. The morning fields of berries, apples, grapes, the sun lifting itself proudly over the alluvial riches of Portugal—it all felt now like a prelude, a softening, a preparation.

Everywhere I went, someone carried a story about the Templars. A secret passage they had sealed beneath a church. A forgotten outpost they once manned. A lover they whispered about in backroom taverns. A relic moved under the cover of night. And though I listened politely, nodding as though these tales were harmless folklore, some deeper chamber of my soul vibrated each time the order was mentioned. For I was following not simply the pilgrimage of St. James now—I was walking parallel to an older, more enigmatic current. A current that had been pulling at me ever since I first read of the mahogany caravel wrecked off Australian shores. That lone fragment of foreign timber—dark, sacred, impossible—felt like a message cast forward through centuries. A grail in the midst of longing for answers to the mystery. A vessel carrying the memory of men who lived halfway between religion and rebellion.

And here I was, walking along their old river sentry routes, the Tejo shimmering like an unbroken silver thread connecting my steps to theirs. Yet beneath all that fascination with myth, with knights and caravels and secret histories, I sensed another truth trying to reach me. A truth I had not been ready to hear on my first Camino, nor on my second—inner alchemy.
The quiet, relentless work of becoming the man I had always been meant to be. But transformation is inconvenient. It asks for your illusions first. And so the Camino—ever the patient teacher—made sure to give me both: a quest to distract me, and a desire to expose me.

For I knew, as I climbed the steep road into **Santarém**, thighs burning, pack digging into my shoulders, that the real reason my thoughts strayed so often back to Porto had nothing to do with architecture or port wine. It had everything to do with the woman who had kissed me on the boundary of Lisbon. Her smile still hovered in my memory—the playful arch of her eyebrow, the brilliant mind behind her musings on Portuguese history, and her curiosity about my own origins. Even now, days later, I could still feel the warmth of her breath when she leaned close to translate a street sign or point out a hidden church linked to the Templars' old patrol lines.

She had driven me to the city's edge with a tenderness that appeared almost accidental. But I knew better. Such moments are never accidents on pilgrimage. Her kiss lingered like a promise. Her absence lingered like a test.

And as I walked northward, step after dusty step, I felt the push and pull of her presence in my body—desire, distraction, longing, and an unnerving sense that she seemed to symbolise something far beyond romance. She was the embodiment of the life force I had suppressed for years. The flame I had buried under grief. The passion I had convinced myself I no longer deserved. She was the living proof that I was not done yet.

And so, when the rooftops of Porto finally rose into view— layered tiles climbing the hillside, the Douro River cutting a path of molten gold through the heart of the city—I felt a surge of emotion rise in me like a tide.

I descended through the narrow streets toward the riverfront, the smell of grilled fish and sweet pastries drifting through the air. As I turned the final corner toward the station where we had arranged to meet, my heart betrayed me—quickening, tightening, opening. I saw her before she saw me. Standing near the entrance, hair lifted by the wind, her eyes scanning the crowd with a searching softness that seemed almost out of place in the bustle of commuters. For a moment, I simply watched her, unnoticed, as though witnessing an apparition that had stepped out of the pages of my own unfinished story. When her gaze finally met mine, everything else—the Templars, the shipwreck legend, the symbol of the mahogany hull, my private inner alchemy—fell momentarily silent.

When she reached me, she placed a hand on my chest—over my heart—and said softly, "You look different. Changed."
I did not know how to answer, for she spoke a truth I had not yet admitted to myself. But the Camino had changed me. And this woman had awakened parts of me that had been asleep far too long. For the first time on this third Camino, I felt something inside me surrender. Not to her, but to the journey itself. To what it was shaping me into. To the truth I had been circling for years, unaware. This Camino was not about uncovering the secret of a ship. It was uncovering the secret of myself.

We found a small pension room overlooking **the Douro**, its window shutters faded by decades of sun and sea air. The city hummed below—trams, laughter, the clink of glasses—yet the moment the door closed behind us, Porto disappeared.

What followed was inevitable. It was fierce.Urgent.A collision rather than a union. Her lips pressed against mine with a hunger that matched my own, two bodies drawn together not by love but by a mutual longing to escape the hollowness each carried. Passion surged into every corner of that room. For a time, the ache of grief dissolved. For a time, the world narrowed to skin, breath, and the trembling electricity of touch. But when the fire subsided, and silence settled around us like a heavy cloak, the truth crept back—quiet but unmistakable.

I lay beside her, her head resting on my shoulder, and knew with painful clarity: This was not love. It was an anesthetic. A temporary balm over a wound that only surrender to God could heal. The passion had not filled the void—it had only illuminated how vast that void had become.

She slept, peaceful and untroubled, while I stared at the dark ceiling. And in that stillness, the Camino whisper stirred inside me. You cannot substitute the divine with desire. You cannot outrun the grief in another's arms. You must walk through what you fear.

I rose early, careful not to wake her, and went down to the river. The morning mist hovered over the Douro like a veil. Boats bobbed quietly, their hulls reflecting the soft dawn light —mahogany, dark and ancient-looking, the very colour of the driftwood piece that had set this quest ablaze.
The grail symbolism washed over me again—the caravel as a sacred vessel, a bearer of hidden knowledge, a reminder that treasure is not discovered but revealed. And I knew then: my fascination with the ship had been my mind's way of avoiding the deeper call—a distraction wrapped in the cloak of purpose.

The Templars. The caravels.The mysterious wreck on the Australian shores. Even the Portuguese woman. Each was an outward symbol of the inward treasure I had not yet surrendered to.

When she joined me at the riverside café later that morning, the air between us carried both the sweetness of the night before and the discomfort of an unspoken truth. She held my arm tightly as we wandered through the streets of Porto—past **São Bento Station,** through Ribeira, up toward the cathedral—and for moments at a time, I let myself believe the illusion that we were meant for one another. Her presence grounded me: the way she explained old myths, the stories she carried in her scholar's mind, the depth in her eyes when she spoke of history as though she had lived it. But she also challenged me, for the closeness stirred things I had not resolved—fragile remnants of grief, shadows of longing, the unearthed fear of loving again only to lose again. Something inside me grew restless.

Love in Hindsight.

The Camino had always been a teacher in motion, and the more I stayed still in Porto—wrapped in the warmth of her company—the more the path pulled at my feet, urging me onward. We visited a Templar site on the outskirts of the city, its stone walls cool and echoing, the air thick with the ghost of prayers. She spoke of the order with reverence, of their guardianship of pilgrims, of their role in shaping the spiritual veins of Portugal. I listened, but my heart was elsewhere—caught between her hand entwined with mine and the unspoken truth that our paths were never meant to merge.

By afternoon, irritation crept in at the edges of my affection. The Portuguese lover's closeness felt suddenly heavy, like a cloak that wasn't mine to wear. She sensed it, of course—women always sense these shifts. She asked softly, "Are you alright?" And I lied. "Just tired." But the Camino knew. God knew. The truth is known.

That night, we lay together again, but something had changed. The passion felt muted, strained by an undercurrent neither of us dared name. I felt the Camino calling me back to solitude, to prayer, to the inner work I had avoided for too long.

In the morning, I rose early again. The room felt too small, too filled with possibilities that were never meant to be realised. As I strapped my pack, the goddess watched me silently from the bed, her eyes clouded with unspoken questions. We kissed goodbye at the bridge—her lips lingering a moment longer than mine—and then I stepped back onto the Camino. And though she would remain in my life long after the pilgrimage ended, lingering like the aftertaste of a strong wine, the relationship had been doomed from the beginning. A passionate detour. A necessary error. A fire that illuminated, rather than warmed.

The Camino had redirected me. Through desire. Through discomfort. Through the ache of letting go. For the road ahead demanded more than passion. It demanded surrender. The painful kind. The transformative kind. The kind the other two Caminos had tried to teach me, but I had not yet been awake enough to understand.

Leaving Porto behind me should have felt like a liberation, yet for the first few kilometres, it felt like tearing off a bandage that wasn't fully healed beneath it. The early light spilled across the pavement, catching the blue azulejo tiles of village chapels and small houses—those sacred mosaics of Portuguese life. But my mind was not on tiles or chapels; it was on her. Love had not bound us. But longing had. And longing can be as deceptive as any illusion the mind conjures. Every step away from the city tugged at that thin thread of desire, the irrational part of me that clung to the warm fantasy of companionship—her laughter over wine, her fierce intelligence, her body entwined with mine under the night air of the Douro. But beneath that was another truth: The Camino was pulling me away from her even as she drew closer. Her presence illuminated my brokenness rather than healing it. The more she tried to intertwine her life with mine, the more I felt the Camino whispering: You must walk alone. You must surrender the substitute for the Source. You must let go of what was never meant to hold you.

Her questions about the caravel, the Templars, and my purpose —they no longer fueled my quest. Instead, they felt like distractions from the deeper current rising within me. A current that demanded honesty. A current that demanded letting go. We made love again, but it felt different— as though the Camino was holding up a mirror, showing me that what I sought in her arms was what I had denied in God's.

And the more I clung, the more I felt my spirit pulled toward inevitable truth: This relationship was born out of longing, not love. It was a bridge, not a destination. A fire meant to burn away illusion, not warm my future. The Camino was not trying to take her from me. It was trying to give me back to myself.

Eventually—even after the pilgrimage ended—I dragged the relationship far past its natural life, trying to salvage something tender from something fundamentally misaligned. But every attempt only confirmed what the Camino had shown me gently, then firmly: It was passion born of pain. Desire born of loss. A substitute for surrender. A delay in transformation.

And in the end, when it finally collapsed—as all illusions must—I could see clearly what I could not see then: It was necessary. It was part of the third awakening. It was the fire that cleared the ground for surrender.

The day I left the Portuguese woman behind for the final time was not marked by any dramatic farewell or emotional punctuation point. It ended, as illusions often do, with a quiet exhale — more a release than a rupture. She stood at the station platform, eyes soft, hopeful perhaps, or resigned. I kissed her cheek gently. There was no fire left, no ache, only a tenderness shaped by gratitude and a surprising calm.

The train carried her northward, and I watched it shrink into a single point of silver light as it climbed into the distance. When the final carriage disappeared, the silence that descended around me felt like the silence after a storm. Clean. Bare. Honest. And in that stillness, I understood: She had never been the destination. She had been the mirror, and the Camino was the truth reflected within it.

It was a *protective detachment* I retreated to—a well-worn cave in my inner world—whenever intimacy collapsed or dissolved, as it had done so many times in my life. Not just in the present relationship, but stretching back through the long corridors of my past. It was always the same pattern: the emotional shutdown, the retreat from vulnerability, the quiet slipping away from the discomfort of being truly seen. And so I survived by mask.

Many masks. Layer upon layer of personality, charm, humour, competence, stoicism—whatever allowed me to navigate the world without exposing the trembling child within. These masks carried me through decades. They kept the pain at bay. They allowed me to function—even succeed—while my deeper self remained hidden behind doors I dared not open. But now, in my older years, in the softening that comes with age and the hard truths that refuse to be silenced, the reality of the Self looms larger than ever. The child within—that boy who had been silenced by trauma, who had learned to swallow grief, to bury longing, to "cope" instead of truly feel—began to cry. And his cry was not gentle. It was the agonising cry of truth breaking through a lifetime of defence. A cry that deflated the ego-self instantly. No mask could withstand it. Except one. The Mask of Christ. Not the mask of dogma. Not the mask of religiosity. But the one mask that was not a mask at all.

For when I put on that Mask— when I looked at my life, my wounds, my failures and my longing through His face—I found I could not lie, not to myself, and not to others. His mask was transparent. It stripped me to the bone. It revealed my fears, my hunger for love, my misplaced desires, my unhealed wounds.

It showed me that what I had long mistaken for passion was often a longing to fill the unfillable: the ache of the soul for God. Looking back on my second Camino, and now stepping toward the Third, I realised that this unveiling of the Self— this tearing away of masks—was not a failure, but a calling. The Camino had been showing me all along that the states of wandering, the passionate entanglements that promised salvation but delivered confusion, the restless seeking for home in a woman's arms, the avoidance of inner alchemy, the refusal to surrender—were not detours. They were *preparations*. Preparations for a deeper stripping. Preparations for a more complete surrender. Preparations for letting go— and letting God.

For it is one thing to walk the Camino with your feet. It is another thing entirely to walk it with your soul. And the dawning realisation— quiet but undeniable—was this: Christ-like suffering is not a punishment. It is a doorway. A passage into rebirth. A preparation for a real pilgrimage —the inner Camino—the one that does not end at the Cathedral in Santiago but begins there.

The Camino had led me to this moment of reckoning. Mask by mask, illusion by illusion, the truth was being revealed: That surrender was not the end of the journey—it was the beginning.

I adjusted the straps of my pack, turtrail, and exhaled as though my soul had dropped twenty kilos in a moment. The wind carried the scent of eucalyptus and wet earth. A familiar rhythm returned to my feet. And the ache of longing was replaced by a subtle anticipation — the unmistakable call of Galicia.

The Portuguese landscape gradually shifted. Vineyards loosened, the air grew cooler, and the forest tracks thickened with moss. And then came the first whispers of what lay beyond the frontier — that ancient land where the Celts had once danced around fire, where Christianity grew not by force but by fusion, blending with the older earth-religions like wine poured into water.

Galicia. A place where witchcraft was not evil, only misunderstood. A place where St. James preached not to conquer but to transform. A place where the sacred and the superstitious walked hand in hand, just as I now walked with my own shadow and awakening. Crossing the long bridge into Galicia was not a simple geographic shift. It was a crossing of inner thresholds. The air thickened with meaning. The forests darkened with memory. And then the mists came. Soft at first, curling around treetops, slipping across the path like ghosts of pilgrims who had walked before me. I felt suddenly accompanied — not by people, but by something ancient, something that had been waiting.

I whispered aloud without fully knowing why: "I'm ready."

The climb toward **O Cebreiro** was steep, demanding, and almost punishing. But the reward — that exquisite moment of cresting the ridge and seeing Galicia spread before me in folds of green and grey — struck me like an echo of my first Camino—a déjà vu wrapped in revelation.

On my first pilgrimage, I had arrived here blistered, naïve, carried partly by adrenaline, partly by awe. On my second, I had trudged through merciless heat, driven more by will than wonder. But on this third inward Camino, walking through memory rather than miles, I saw clearly what I had missed: Both earlier journeys had been preparation. Only now was I truly awake enough to understand.

As I descended the winding path toward **Triacastela** — that sacred valley of chestnut forests and whispering water — the memories of walking with Young, of composing poems, of cooling aching feet in mountain streams, rose around me like spectral companions. But now they were not memories. They were teachers. Every bend of the pathway whispered: *"Look again. What you thought you were walking toward was always walking toward you."*

The legends of Galicia seemed to animate themselves in the shadows — the *meigas*(witch-women) of the medieval hillsides, the early Christian converts of St. James, the Celts who revered the wind and the fire. Their stories folded into my own until I could no longer tell where history ended, and my inner mythology began. The Camino was no longer a journey across a country. It was a journey across the map of my soul.

By the time **Triacastela** appeared, nestled at the bottom of the valley like a secret kept by the mountains, I knew with certainty: I was walking not for the woman, not for the Templars, not for the caravel, but for the surrender I had always resisted.

My first Camino cracked me open. My second Camino stripped me bare. This third Camino — the inner one — invited me to step fully into what waited beneath the stripping. I had been seeking treasure in the world. Now I understood: The treasure was the transformation itself.
And **Galicia** — mystical, shadowed, green —was the crucible where that transformation began to take form.

And yet, even in that brief season of union, even in the fire of our bodies meeting as though they had always been meant to collide, I felt the truth moving underneath like a quiet undertow: this was not love. It was longing wearing the mask of intimacy. It was the ancient ache of the heart seeking to fill its own hollowness with the warmth of another body, another promise, another face. It was the exhausted soul reaching for comfort rather than surrender. And in those moments—moments where the passion was real, undeniable, consuming —I already knew that its foundation was trembling. The very intensity of the desire revealed the wound it was trying to conceal. I had run into her arms like a man fleeing a burning house. But she was not the sanctuary I was seeking. She was the distraction from the sanctuary. And yet—God forgive me —I *needed* that distraction then. The grief that shadowed me was still sharp, still unintegrated. And the Camino, with its dusty roads and ancient stones, had offered me her as though testing me, as though asking gently: "Will you surrender to pain—or sedate it?" The answer was obvious. I took the sedative. But the Camino never punishes. It *reveals.*

I did not know then how deeply the symbolism of the Grail—my "caravan," the quest I had been circling for years—was quietly shaping this encounter in Porto. That mythic cup, that vessel of divine union, had become inverted in my hands. Instead of holding the sacred, I had filled it with longing and called it destiny. I had mistaken intensity for truth.

Her presence in Porto both steadied and unsettled me. She grounded me with her warmth, with her laughter, with the easy way she reached for my hand when crossing a street.

And when it finally ended, the Grail symbol—my "caravan"—stood before me again, emptied this time, ready to be filled with something real, something earned, something sacred.

Resignation was the beginning of the third Camino, long before my feet touched the earth of Spain again—a Camino of surrender. A Camino of truth. A Camino of becoming awake to what had been invisible on the first and second. The Third Camino lacked a starting point on a map. It did not begin in Lisbon, nor in St-Jean, nor on the descent into Triacastela. It began in the marrow of my being—in the quiet place where the truth can no longer be negotiated with. By the time I recognised that I was already undertaking the Third Camino, I had travelled thousands of kilometres on foot, but millions more within myself.

The first Camino had broken me open. The second had shown me the masks I still clung to. But the third…the third came like a whisper, like a calling, like a soft but relentless hand guiding me into a rebirth I had resisted all my life. This Camino was not out there. It was *in here*.

God in plain sight.

The earlier pilgrimages, beautiful and painful as they were, had all been rehearsals—sacred dress rehearsals—for the moment when the true stripping would begin. At first, I did not understand this. I thought the Third Camino would simply be another trek, another attempt to resolve something through motion, another escape into the arms of a woman, another quest for a relic, a Templar secret, a mythic Grail in hopes that it would soothe the unrest within me. But the truth was clearer now, painfully clear: The Grail I had been chasing was not a cup. Nor a shipwreck. Nor a lost treasure. It was the Self I had been too afraid to confront.

No, this was entirely different. I was being transformed unconsciously; unlike the outer Caminos, the inner one could not be avoided, walked around, or disguised by passion, lust, or mythology. An in my awakening on route, it came to me The Third Camino confronted me with what I had avoided for decades: Loneliness, Longing. Loss. The deep ache for love that no woman—no matter how desired—could truly remedy. The emptiness that had shaped my life's choices.
The child within, abandoned and silenced. And the man who had survived by fleeing into masks. All of it.

And so the likeness to Christ came not as a theological idea. but as a lived reality. Jesus homelessness. Jesus rejection. His vulnerability. His longing for companionship, yet the misunderstanding of those closest to Him. His suffering at the hands of the world and His surrender to something greater.

I saw myself in that story—not in glory, but in ache. I had written it from deep within my creative self. Foxes have holes and birds have nests, but this Son of Man has nowhere to rest" I had lived that line. I had sung it into my own composition, *Lead Kindly Light*, long before I fully understood it. For my entire life, I had wandered—from relationship to relationship, from quest to quest, from Camino to Camino—seeking a place to rest my head, a home for my heart. But all along, God had been whispering: *"Your suffering is not your enemy. It is your teacher. It is the crucible in which you will finally be reborn."*

And this was the grace the Third Camino revealed: That surrender is not capitulation. It is the release of illusion. The acceptance that no one out there can heal the wound within.
That Christ-like suffering is not a punishment but the doorway, the gate, the portal through which the soul enters new life.

Acceptance of my lot was the pilgrimage I had resisted for too long. The one without a guidebook. The one with no cafés, no albergues, no companions to distract me from myself. The one where every step echoed inward, and every silence became a mirror.
And finally— finally— I began to understand: The Camino is not walked to Santiago. It is walked from Santiago onward— into the inner sanctuary, into the place where God and Self meet, into the long-awaited rebirth of soul.
I remember it now, though for years I pretended I did not. The moment had been quiet, almost ordinary, easy to overlook in the haze of exhaustion and emotion of that first arrival into Santiago. The little priest—short in stature, silver-haired and soft-spoken—had delivered his homily first in rolling Spanish, and then, for the benefit of the many foreign pilgrims, he

repeated it slowly in English. At the time I heard his words, but only with half a heart. I was too overwhelmed, too relieved, too fractured to receive them. They slipped past my conscious mind, like seeds falling unnoticed into soil that had not yet been tilled. But now—years later, after the second Camino, after the missteps of Lisbon and Porto, after the cycles of longing, illusion, heartbreak, masks, collapse, and awakening—his voice returned. **Not in memory alone. It rose** from somewhere *beneath* memory, from the deep well of the subconscious where truth waits.

I heard him again, clearly, almost as if he were standing at my shoulder on the Portuguese Way: "You have walked your pilgrimage through the night of the soul into the light.
Now it is time to live. Really live." Back then, I nodded politely, as a pilgrim does. I thought he meant, "Go home and enjoy life."I thought he meant celebration, achievement, a happy ending. I did not fully understand that he was speaking of rebirth, of a life not built from the old self but born from its ashes.

And so, unknowingly, I buried his blessing. I walked away from the Cathedral still carrying my old patterns, my old fears, my old hunger for external redemption. Only now—after the unravelling of two Caminos, after the Portuguese woman, after the collapse of illusions, after the masks fell away—did I see what he had really spoken into me. A seed. A charge. A quiet prophecy. To live was not to chase after passions symbolically or quests.
To live was to allow the dying—the surrender—the Christ-like descent into the places within me I feared most. To live was to walk not to Santiago, but into myself. It had taken years, three

pilgrimages, failed love, a spiritual breakdown, and the long wandering of my heart to realise the seed had sprouted. The priest's voice—so small, so gentle—was now thundering through my third Camino. And the memory rekindled thoughts of my visit to **Fatima.**

Memories of the apparitions and their mysteries, towards another layer of my own unfolding. The seed planted was awakening. And with it, the next historic recall of my journey was about to begin.

The priest's words lingered long after the memory of them faded into silence. They became like an underground stream, moving quietly beneath the noise of my life—beneath the passionate entanglements, the quests for hidden ships and Grail symbols, the longing to be held, the fear of being seen, the masks I perfected just to survive my own history. And as the third Camino unfolded beneath my feet, his voice returned, soft yet unmistakably insistent: "You have come through the night. Now it is time to live." But living—truly living—meant something far different now than it ever had. It no longer meant worldly adventure, or romance, or chasing mysteries across continents. It meant walking, finally, into the one territory I had avoided even on pilgrimage: my own soul.

And so, with that voice echoing through me, I found myself being drawn back toward Fátima—a place I had previously approached with curiosity, detachment, even scepticism.

But now something deeper stirred.

Fátima was not merely another waypoint on the map. It was not a tourist site, nor a Catholic relic to admire from a distance. It was a threshold—a place where suffering, mystery, and revelation converged—not unlike my own inner landscape. I remembered the stories of the three shepherd children, the visions, the secrets whispered to them by a woman clothed in light. The first two secrets had already unfolded in history—war, revolution, devastation. The third, sealed in the Vatican vaults for decades, had fuelled speculation, prophecy, and fear.

In thinking about this now, the truth was, I was not seeking the secrets of Fátima. I was seeking my own. And something in me sensed that the outer mysteries were merely mirrors of the inner ones.

The closer I drew to the sanctuary, the more I felt a strange convergence: my Christian roots, my yearning for transformation, my unhealed wounds, and the remnants of that misguided search for love in the arms of the Portuguese woman. All of it was rising now, meeting in a single point of tension—as if Fátima itself were calling me to a reckoning. It was not the Virgin's secrets I would confront there. It was my own resistance, my uncried tears, my unwillingness to surrender completely, my longing for God tangled with my fear of being seen by Him. Fátima would strip me. Not of possessions or illusions of romance or quests for lost caravels —those had already been taken. Fátima would strip me of the last mask: the belief that I could walk this path half-awake, half-surrendered, half-trusting.

As I approached the shrine, walking the long colonnades where pilgrims crawled on their knees toward the chapel of apparitions, I felt a trembling, a vulnerability, a softness breaking open in me. The journey was no longer the Camino of my youth, nor the Camino of my distractions. The Way here was the Camino of the heart laid bare. And I sensed—just as the priest's blessing had foretold—that something was about to begin living in me that had long been asleep. A birth through fire. A surrender through silence. A grace that had followed me from Santiago, waited through Lisbon and Porto, and now a presence at the gates of Fátima, inviting me to enter.

So it was that I recalled the mystery of my journey to Fátima, aware of a deep need within me to investigate the secrets of Our Lady's revelations. At the same time, I was conscious of my doubts—particularly my hesitation to believe in beings from another world—yet confronted by the fact that at least two of the three secrets had seemingly materialised, unfolding much as those three children had foretold.

Though I had been indoctrinated from youth to believe in God, the Virgin Mary, and the suffering and death of Christ, the circumstances of my life had begun to erode that certainty. I found myself questioning whether it was, in fact, all a myth— whether my beliefs had been shaped by those in religious authority, filling our minds with stories that granted them power over the faithful and rules we were expected to live by. It led me to wonder if much of what I had accepted as truth— my thoughts, my feelings, even my sense of reality—was, to a significant degree, constructed rather than real.

My journey, I realised, was altogether different from what I had imagined—and in that recognition, there was a strange kind of truth. So, despite my more worldly longings, my romantic notions, and my fascination with history and legend, Fátima became for me an essential pilgrimage: a place where I might either reaffirm or relinquish my inner faith, and with it, my belief in God and in humanity itself.

Yet as I reflected more deeply, I began to see the tangible outcomes that had emerged from the experiences of those simple, saintly children who claimed visions of Mary. Their message was not one of grandeur, but of humility: to pray the rosary, to make restitution through penance and sacrifice, and to accept suffering as part of the path toward redemption— away from both earthly destruction and eternal loss.

There was, too, the unsettling claim that they had foretold events such as the Second World War and the tensions of the Cold War that followed, with Russia playing a pivotal role in either peace or devastation, depending on humanity's response through prayer. And curiously, elements of this seemed to have taken shape—particularly in places like the United States, where vast numbers gathered daily in prayer, united through radio and global movements centred on the rosary as a plea for peace.

Whether by coincidence, faith, or something beyond understanding, it left me suspended between belief and doubt —yet unable to entirely dismiss what I had seen, heard, and felt.

On my visit, I recall being viscerally moved by the sheer throng of people gathered in prayer in the great square before the altar, standing before the statue of Mary—set in stone, a direct representation of how the children had described her. There were simply too many people for me to remain there long, so I made my way to the small chapel and visited the tombs of the three children of Fátima. Two had died not long after the apparitions, and Lúcia, who had become a nun, had only recently passed and was buried there as well.

As it happened, an Irish priest and a lay nun knelt before the children's graves, receiving and reciting a mystery of the Rosary, and I felt compelled to join them. It was a quiet, intimate moment—one that seemed to exist outside of time.

Of course, it had no connection to my later return to Lisbon, where I would meet the Portuguese woman again and continue our troubled relationship. It would ultimately take the death of my passion for her before I returned home to Australia, a wounded soul in need of healing. Yet I had learned much from my time at Fátima—not only of spiritual devotion, but also of the ways of the world that seemed to move quietly alongside it.

Looking for Fatima

Calling at the station
Asking at the square
Nobody knew of Fatima
Nobody seemed to care.

There's an in-depth resignation.
To the state of that affair,
People fighting for survival
There are no angels here.

Show me the coin of the realm
Heard some sage just say,
It's all about to crumble,
The euros fading away.

It will take a mighty crumb.
Castle walls just won't remain,
It will take more than the IMF
For Fatima to stand.

Pilgrims look in plenty.
Praying for their upkeep,
No money in their pockets,
No one is counting sheep.

Looking for Fatima.
Searching for Fatima

Pilgrims give sweet charity.
To the Lady, they offer prayers,
When the walls crumble to rubble
Will Fatima still stand?

No one is paying attention.
To the corners of the mind,
so busy turning tricks
No way can they find.

Caught a bus to Fatima,
To visit the Virgin Mary,
All I saw was a statue,
a riddle to solve a myth.

She stood there at the altar
A beauty in a white dress,
with a foot upon a serpent,
She forgave my ignorance.

Now she wears for me
a crown of Stars,
And rides upon the Moon.
For the queen of hearts is love.

Looking for Fatima,
Searching for Fatima.

Time and Tide.

A flash of memory returns—my final steps to **Finisterre,** once believed in medieval times to be the end of the earth. The wild ocean crashed angrily upon the shore, sending great sprays of water high into the air, only to recede again as if searching for peace—before rising once more in its eternal, restless rhythm.

I recall the climb of that final kilometre to the zero marker of the Camino, where I stood and gazed across the vast oceanscape. In a sweeping, almost 180-degree vision, I looked back toward Finisterre, the fishing village steeped in legend—where it is said that St. James once stood in despair at his failure to ignite belief in Christ across the Iberian Peninsula. And then, as the story goes, the Virgin Mary appeared to him —still alive in her earthly life—asking him to build a church in her honour at Muxía, overlooking that rugged and beautiful coast. She came as "Our Lady of the Boat," and from that moment, faith began to take root, turning hearts from ancient beliefs toward the teachings of Christ.

Later, I walked back down the steep incline toward the ocean, alone and in a state of inner flux. It was there that I encountered something that felt like a fragment of time itself, drifting in on the tide. As I had once done at Long Reef back in Australia, I waded into the water. In that moment, I realised I had fulfilled one of those long-held, almost foolish quests— the mystery of the mahogany ship said to have been wrecked on the coast of Victoria. Yet it felt empty. Like so many of the goals I had pursued, it offered no lasting meaning—only the hollow echo of desire. A vision came to me of Moses descending the mountain with the Ten Commandments, while below, the people worshipped idols. I saw myself in that image—chasing material aims, romantic illusions, distant grails—each one slipping through my hands like sand falling onto parched earth. The mirror image of the Long Reef Maghony timbered realm I left there on the beach at Finisterre.

I made my way then to the rocky edge of the ocean near **Muxía.** In one hand, I held the note from the woman I had carried since my first Camino; in the other, the crucifix given to me by Brother John of the Order of Mother Teresa. And as you, the reader, may recall, I had begun this story for some future soul—someone who might one day turn this journey into a film, using its signposts and songs as stepping stones along the way.

So it was, in that moment, that I stood facing the sea and let the note go. The wind caught it and carried it outward, across the water. It was more than a gesture—it was a release. Not only of the women, the illusions, and the last of them, the Portuguese lover, but of the material world itself. I saw clearly then the futility of trying to force myself, a square peg, into the round hole of that world.

And then—as if already written into the script of the story—I turned and saw a young man, a pilgrim not unlike my former self, standing there with tears in his eyes, staring out to sea. In that suspended moment, I placed the crucifix into his hand, just as Brother John had once given it to me, and said quietly: "Jesus will guide you."

And with that, this pilgrim—this self-fashioned adventurer of the Camino—turned and walked away into the mist. As I imagined it, the scene would fade… and the credits would begin to roll, carried by the distant but rising sound of a song I had written: *Teach the Children.*

It is in transformation. It is to walk among others with humility, to carry no need for recognition, and to become, in whatever small way we can, a light for those still searching.
Not by words. It is by letting go—a soft surrender of all that no longer serves us.

It is here, perhaps, that the journey truly comes into its own—not as a path to somewhere, but as a return to what was always within us. Beneath the striving, beneath the longing, beneath the illusions we once held so tightly. What remains is simple. To love without possession. To give without expectation. To walk without needing to arrive.
And in that simplicity, something profound begins to emerge—not something new, but something that was always there, waiting quietly beneath the surface of who we thought we had to be. Perhaps that is what this story has been all along. Not just an adventure, nor merely a reflection, but an invitation.

An invitation for the reader, like the pilgrim, to see their own life in a different light—not as a series of pursuits, but as a journey of becoming. A journey that may lead, as it did for me, through longing and loss, through illusion and awakening… until, at last, there is nothing left to chase.
Only something to live. And in that living, to become what, perhaps, we were always destined to be. The Camino doesn't ask to leave the world behind. It asks something far more difficult—that we learn to live within it without being consumed by it.

For much of my life, I had chased the things the world told me were important: love, success, meaning, identity. And in doing so, I had become entangled in them, mistaking their pursuit for purpose. The Camino, in its quiet and persistent way, did not strip these things from me—it simply revealed their true weight. And in that revelation came a choice. To continue as before… or to begin again, differently.

There is a spiritual essence to the journey, yes—but it is not found in outward displays, nor in the myths and legends that surround it, nor in the stories of saints, nor even in the footsteps of those who walked before us. These may guide us, inspire us, even draw us to the path—but they are not the destination.

The true Camino begins when those things fall away.
When we come to understand that to "live in this world, but not be of it" is not an act of withdrawal, but of quiet transformation. It is to walk among others with humility, to carry no need for recognition, and to become, in whatever small way we can, a light for those still searching, not by words, but by how we live.

For the young, the Camino may well be a rite of passage—an adventure, a testing of the body and spirit, something that should indeed be encouraged. But for those of us who have walked longer roads, who have seen more of life and carry its weight, it becomes something else entirely—a reckoning. A letting go.—a soft surrender of all that no longer serves us.
It is here, perhaps, that the journey truly comes into its own—not as a path to somewhere, but as a return to what was always within us. Beneath the striving, beneath the longing, beneath

the illusions we once held so tightly. What remains is simple. To love without possession. To give without expectation. To walk without needing to arrive.

And in that simplicity, something profound begins to emerge —not something new, but something that was always there, waiting quietly beneath the surface of who we thought we had to be. Perhaps that is what this story has been all along. Not just an adventure, nor merely a reflection, but an invitation. An invitation for the reader, like the pilgrim, to see their own life in a different light—not as a series of pursuits, but as a journey of becoming. A journey that may lead, as it did for me, through longing and loss, through illusion and awakening… until, at last, there is nothing left to chase. Only something to live. And in that living, to become what, perhaps, we were always destined to be.

Meditate upon this vision.
Peace and calm are the quest.
Clear the mind of former glory.
We and nature need a rest.

It's the sign of a new beginning
The changes coming through
Shaking off the chains that bind us
We're learning to renew.

Feel the earth beneath your feet.
Hear the mighty ocean roar.
Climb a mountain in your mind.
Look down on the valley floor.

Teach the children
The ways of nature
Teach the children
How to grow.

Teach the children
The ways of nature
It's by example that we show.

Peace and calm are our mantra.
Love and joy we sing about
Asking for the God of mercy
Renew our world, let it ring out.

In the silence of the moment
Before the cock begins to crow
We rejoice in the presence
Of twlights eternal glow.

Feel the earth beneath your feet.
Hear the mighty ocean roar.
Climb a mountain in your mind.
Look down on a valley floor.

Teach the children
The ways of nature
Teach the children
How to grow.

Teach the children
The ways of nature
It's by example
That's what we show.

Feel the spirit of the Higher Power.
In a moment of release
Trusting in his grace and mercy
To heal the earth and bring us peace.

Clear the mind of former glory,
Calm it all, let it be still
Breathing in deep presence
Spirit soul is guiding will.

Teach the children
The ways of nature
Teach the children
How to grow.

Teach the children
The ways of nature
It's by example
That we show.

And so, dear reader, if I were to sum up this story of my introspective Quest, it would speak volumes more as a film than what I can portray here. I trust that someday a visionary soul will take up the mantle of this story where I have left off. Maybe, before turning to film, they might read the many books of the Camino I have written to find the spiritual essence of the Camino for those who follow.

The Quest is the story of an outward pilgrimage that becomes an inward awakening, where the road to Santiago mirrors the soul's search for meaning, healing, and truth. Its vision is to remind readers that life's deepest purpose lies not in worldly success but in authenticity, humility, compassion, and a reconnection with the sacred. Its songs, carried through poetic reflections, speak of longing, struggle, surrender, gratitude, and redemption—the timeless melody of the human heart seeking home.

Film Script: The Quest.

Scene 1: The Ascent

Location: The Pyrenees (Route de Napoléon). Visual: High-altitude wide shots. A lone PILGRIM (60s, weathered but steady) climbs against a backdrop of mist and jagged peaks. The wind is the only sound until the music swells. Audio: "The Quest" begins to play. As the tempo builds, the voiceover fades in (from the website www.caminoway.com.au "About Us" page). Voiceover (V.O.): "The Camino is not just a walk; it is a stripping away of the noise until only the soul remains..."

Scene 2: The Catalyst of Youth

Location: The French Way – rolling hills in the background.

Visual: The Pilgrim walks with a group of YOUNGER PILGRIMS. They are laughing, their energy a contrast to the Pilgrim's quiet contemplation. Audio: "Walking the Camino" (Upbeat, rhythmic). Dialogue:

- Young Pilgrim: "Why are you walking now? Why this year?"
- Pilgrim: (Smiling) "Because the road doesn't ask if you're ready. It just waits." Transition: The scene fades to a candlelit chapel. The music shifts to "Lead Kindly Light." The Pilgrim kneels. Herevin is the moment of decision—the bridge between his past life and this walk.

Scene 3: The Garden of Memory

Location: A lush, familiar garden (Flashback). Visual: Soft focus. The Pilgrim walks through a stretch of garden that looks like home. He touches a flower. Memories of a past love surface. Audio: "Magdalene" plays softly. Internal Monologue (V.O.): "We seek the Virgin at the end of the road, but we find her in every memory of love we left behind.

Vusaual: A fading sequence of two people in a loving embrace, silhouetted against the background as the scene fades.

" Action: The Pilgrim returns to the dusty trail, his pace matching the song 'Love."

Scene 4: The Miracle at Fatima

Location: Sanctuary of Fátima, Portugal. Visual: A sharp cut to the past: The Portuguese Camino. The Pilgrim stands in the vast square where the three children saw the vision. Audio: "Fatima" (Orchestral/Devotional). Action: The Pilgrim crosses the square on his knees, reflecting the devotion of those around him. He looks at the statue of the Virgin, then back to his present-day scallop shell as he passes another milestone along The Way.

Scene 5: The Walking Monk

Location: Meseta – The Endless Road. Visual: A dusty, flat stretch. The Pilgrim encounters BROTHER JOHN (from The Sword of Discernment). John wears the simple robes of the Brothers of Mother Teresa. He walks with sandals and a white robe shimmering in the early morning light. Audio: "Santiago Traveller."

Scene 6: The Waypoints

Visual Montage: 1. Santo Domingo: Sharing bread with a circle of pilgrims. Laughter over blistered feet. 2. Leon Cathedral: The Pilgrim looks up at the stained glass; the light bathes him in blue and red. 3. The Climb to Foncebadon: Straining against the slope.   The physical toll of the journey. 4. The Iron Cross at Cruz Ferro. Memory of A GUITARIST sits by the cross, playing a haunting acoustic version of "The Boundary Rider."

[This next section of the film marks a shift from the solitary, mythic heights of the Pyrenees to the vibrant, social "living laboratory" of the Camino. In Burgos, the Pilgrim's introspection is challenged by the pull of human connection and by the "Spanish Girl," who represents the youth and vitality he discerns within himself.]

ACT III: The City of Stone and Spirit

Scene 8: Entering Burgos

Location: The approach to the Burgos Cathedral. Visual: The Pilgrim enters the city through the massive Arco de Santa María. He looks small against the towering Gothic spires. The transition is sharp—from the quiet forests of Zubiri to the echoing stone plazas and the hum of city life. Audio: A lively, guitar-heavy intro to "Walking the Camino."

- Spanish Girl: "You look like you are carrying the whole history of the road in that notebook."

- Pilgrim: "It's a diary. A way to make sure I don't lose the moments."
- Spanish Girl: (Laughing) "The road doesn't want to be kept. It wants to be walked. Look up, Peregrino! The Cathedral is watching us." Director's Note: Use warm, golden-hour lighting. The Pilgrim's face should soften; the "Sword of Discernment" is resting for a moment, replaced by the simple joy of the present.

Scene 10: The Pilgrim Meal (The Communal Table)

Location: A rustic Mesón in the heart of Burgos. Visual: A long wooden table crowded with pilgrims of all nationalities. Bottles of red wine, baskets of bread, and steaming bowls of Sopa de Ajo. Action: The Pilgrim sits next to the Spanish Girl. They are surrounded by the younger pilgrims he met earlier. Audio: The clatter of cutlery and the "Santiago Traveller" melody played on a soft, accordion-style background. V.O. (Pilgrim): "The Diaries speak of the solitude, but the heart remembers the bread. In the breaking of it, we are no longer strangers from different books; we are a single sentence being written by the road."

Scene 11: The Bar – The Laughter of the Way

Location: A narrow, crowded bar in the Calle de San Lorenzo. Visual: The scene is kinetic and loud. The younger pilgrims are drinking cañas, laughing, and singing. The Pilgrim is in the centre of it, caught between his role as an observer (the writer) and a participant (the traveller). Action: The Spanish Girl pulls him into a toast. For a moment, his "Memory Diving" stops. He is fully, vibrantly alive in the "Now." Audio: The music swells into a joyous, percussive bridge. Lyric Overlay: > "Walking the Camino, heart is open wide,

- The Content of the Diaries: This scene draws from the entries about the social Camino—the unexpected friendships that form in a single day and feel like they've lasted a lifetime.
- The Interrelation: In The Sword of Discernment, this moment represents the "Temptation of the Hearth"—the desire to stay in the warmth of human company rather than continuing the solitary spiritual quest.
- Visual Cue: When the Pilgrim looks at the Spanish Girl, the "Familiar Garden" should flash briefly on screen, this time sunny and full of people, indicating that his introspection is moving from "loss" to "connection."

Scene 9: The Girl from the Road (This may come in at scene 9 or be introduced as a flashback, as shown after scene 11.)

Location: The long, flat path leading into the city. Visual: The Pilgrim walks alongside a YOUNG SPANISH GIRL. She carries a light pack and moves with a natural grace. They speak in a mix of Spanish and English. Dialogue can't be distinguished, but add later if required.

The Transition

As the night in the bar fades, the camera should linger on the Pilgrim's diary left on the table, surrounded by wine rings. The next scene will find him leaving the city at dawn, heading toward the silence of the Meseta.

ACT III (Cont.): The Ghost of a Kiss

Scene 12: The Morning Departure

Location: A dimly lit Albergue in Burgos, pre-dawn. Visual: The blue light of 5:00 AM. Pilgrims are whispering and packing in the shadows. Action: The Pilgrim passes the bunk of the SPANISH GIRL. She is asleep, her dark hair splayed across the white pillowcase.

- The Gesture: He pauses. The "Memory Diver" is overcome by a moment of pure, platonic tenderness. He reaches out and gently rustles her hair.
- The Reaction: She stirs, her eyes fluttering open. Recognition dawning, she gives the old pilgrim a sleepy, radiant smile.
- Dialogue (Whispered): * Spanish Girl: "Buen Camino..." Action: He nods, unable to speak, and walks out into the cold morning air.

Scene 13: The Revelation at Hornillos

Location: A small, dusty Albergue in the village of Hornillos del Camino (The first stop on the Meseta). Visual: The Pilgrim is checking in, weary from the day's walk. The Propriotor (an older man with a kind face) examines the Pilgrim's credentials and reads the note in Spanish that the Pilgrim found in his backpack. Action: The Proprietor begins to read, and we see the Spanish writing in and the handwritten translation of the Proprietor

Audio: "Love" begins to play—just the acoustic guitar and a soft cello. Text on Screen/V.O. (Spanish Girl's Voice)

Gracias por ser mi compañero en un día difícil. Te beso."

(Thank you for being my companion on a difficult day. I kiss you.)

The pilgrim looks out towards the vast flat horizon of the Meseta. He touches his chest with the note for his discernment is not just cutting away the bad, it's recognising the weight of a single honest human connection.

ACT IV: The Spiritual Desert

Scene 15: The Meseta – The Infinite Horizon

Location: The high plains between Burgos and Hontanas. Visual: A vast, shimmering sea of wheat and sky. The Pilgrim is a tiny dot moving along a straight line that never seems to end. The dust from his boots rises in slow motion. Audio: "Santiago Traveller" opens with a rhythmic, pulsing beat that mimics the trance-like state of long-distance walking. V.O. (Pilgrim): "The Meseta is the place where the Camino stops being a walk and starts being a surgery. There is nowhere to hide from yourself. No mountains to climb, no forests to shade you. Just you and the Sword.

Scene 16: The Encounter with Brother John

Location: A desolate stretch of trail near Castrojeriz. Visual: A figure appears in the heat haze. It is Brother John again, a monk of the Brothers of Mother Teresa. He walks with a staff, his robes dusty, his gaze terrifyingly peaceful. Action: They walk in silence for a long time. The Pilgrim's diary is tucked away; this is a moment for the pilgrim's Discernment. **Dialogue:**

- Pilgrim: "The silence out here... It's heavy, John."
- Brother John: "It is only heavy because you are trying to carry it. The silence is not a burden; it is the language

of the Creator. You are a 'Santiago Traveller'—but are you travelling toward the Saint, or toward the silence?"

- Pilgrim: "I thought I was walking to find answers."
- Brother John: (Stopping and looking deep into the Pilgrim's eyes) "The Road doesn't give answers. It removes the questions, leaving only the Truth. That is the 'Sword.' It cuts the 'why' out of your heart."

ACT IV (Cont.): The Gift of the Meseta

Scene 16.5: The Parting of Ways

Location: An endless, sun-bleached gravel track on the Meseta. Visual: BROTHER JOHN stops. He stands tall, his silhouette resembling a "David" carved from stone—rugged, powerful, and radiating a stamina that seems supernatural. He reaches into his robes. Action: He places a small, simple Crucifix into the Pilgrim's weathered palm. His hand is steady; the Pilgrim's hand trembles slightly. Dialogue:

- Brother John: (In a voice like deep water) "Take this. When the road gets long, and the silence gets too loud, remember: You are not walking alone. Jesus is guiding you." Action: John doesn't wait for a "thank you." He turns and begins to walk. Visual: John's pace is incredible. Within seconds, he is a receding figure, leaving the "old man pilgrim" standing still in a cloud of fine white dust.

Scene 17: The Solitude of the Cross

Location: The same stretch of road, moments later. Visual: A wide, "god's eye" shot from high above. The Pilgrim is a tiny, solitary point on a line that stretches to infinity. Audio: The music shifts from the rhythmic pulse of "Santiago Traveller" to a solitary, haunting violin. Action: The Pilgrim looks down at the small Crucifix in his hand. He closes his eyes. V.O. (Pilgrim): "John walks with the strength of a man who has already arrived. I walk with the weight of a man still trying to leave. He left me in his dust, but he left me with a compass."

Director's Footnotes: The "David" Motif

- The Content of the Diaries: This reflects the humbling experience of being outpaced on the Camino. It captures the realisation that everyone has their own "speed of spirit."
- The Sword of Discernment * As noted from my book, Brother John is the "Discernment" incarnate. He is the "Sword" that has already been sharpened. By giving the Pilgrim the Crucifix, he is giving him the tool to sharpen his own soul.
- Visual Direction: The "dust" left by Brother John should be filmed in slow motion, catching the light like gold leaf. It symbolises the "Grace" that remains even after the teacher has left. Scene 7: The Ghost of the Past
- Location: A roadside Cafe in Galicia. Visual: The Pilgrim sits alone with a café con leche. A FEMALE PILGRIM from a previous book/walk walks in. Their eyes meet—recognition, regret, and peace. Audio: "Oh! My God." Lyric Overlay: "Oh my God, I see you in the stranger's face..." Action: They don't speak. They simply nod. She moves on. The road claims her.

Scene 18: The Ascent to Foncebadón (The Culmination)

Location: The climb toward the Iron Cross. Visual: The Pilgrim is now moving through the mountains of Leon. He holds the small Crucifix in his hand, pressing it against the top of his staff. Audio: "The Boundary Rider" begins to swell. Action: As he passes the 790km, 500km, 200km markers (in a fast-motion sequence), he encounters the other pilgrims from his journey:

1. He sees the Spanish Girl in a flash of memory, smiling.
2. He hears the Song of Roland in the wind.
3. He feels the weight of the Crucifix. Lyric Overlay: > "The boundary is fading, the fences are down,

I'm no longer lost, I'm no longer bound."

Scene 8: The Arrival

Location: Monte del Gozo, looking toward Santiago de Compostela. Visual: The spires of the Cathedral appear in the distance. A montage of pilgrims from the film—the youth, Brother John, the woman—all walking in slow motion. Audio: "Santiago." Action: The Pilgrim enters the Praza do Obradoiro. He drops his pack. The camera pans up from his worn boots to the Cathedral towers. Final Image: The Pilgrim closes his eyes, a deep breath of arrival. Fade to Black, and a structural breakdown of the remaining scenes, which deepen the connection to your books and music.

Here is the expanded dialogue and a structural breakdown of the remaining scenes, which deepen the connection to your books and music.

Scene 5 Expanded: The Sword of Discernment

Location: The Meseta. The horizon is a flat, shimmering line of heat. Visual: The Pilgrim catches up to BROTHER JOHN. John moves with a rhythmic, effortless gait, despite his heavy robes. The sound of their boots on the gravel creates a steady percussion.

Audio: The intro to "Santiago Traveller" begins—a low, melodic drone that mimics the vastness of the plains.

Dialogue:

- Brother John: (Without looking back) "You are walking with a heavy pack, my friend. But it is not the weight on your shoulders that will tire you; it is the weight of the stories you haven't finished yet."
- Pilgrim: "I've written them all down in diaries, John. I thought putting them on paper would leave them behind."
- Brother John: "The paper is just a map. Discernment is the sword. You must use it to cut through the 'memory-self' to find who is walking now. Every step is a death of the man you were a mile ago."
- Pilgrim: "Is that why you walk? To die to yourself?"
- Brother John: (Stopping to look at the Pilgrim) "I walk because the Camino is a mirror. Some people look in and see a hero; others see a sinner. I hope to look in and see nothing but the Light."

Action: John hands the Pilgrim a simple wooden cross. The music swells as they continue walking, two silhouettes against the immense Spanish sky.

Scene 6: The Waypoints of Faith

The Albergue in Santo Domingo

Visual: Dim light, the smell of woodsmoke and damp wool. The Pilgrim sits at a long table. Action: He watches a group of international pilgrims. They are passing a bottle of wine. The camera focuses on their hands—bruised, dirty, and reaching for one another. V.O. (Pilgrim): "In the breaking of bread, the boundaries of the 'self' begin to blur."

The Cathedral of León

Visual: The Pilgrim stands in the nave. Audio: The ambient echoes of the cathedral. Action: The sun hits the glass, throwing vibrant blues and crimsons onto the Pilgrim's face. He looks at his reflection in a brass plaque. He looks different —thinner, eyes clearer. The "memory diver" is starting to surface.

Foncebadón: The Guitarist

Location: The high, desolate village of Foncebadón. Visual: A lone pilgrim sits on a stone wall, a battered guitar across his lap. Audio: "The Boundary Rider" (Live acoustic version). Action: As the music plays, the Pilgrim approaches the Iron Cross (Cruz de Ferro). He pulls a small stone from his pocket —a stone he has carried since the "familiar garden" of his memories. He places it at the base of the mound. Lyric Overlay: "I'm a boundary rider, checking the fences of my soul..."

Refined Scene 6: Foncebadón and "The Boundary Rider"

Location: The Cruz de Ferro (Iron Cross). The wind is fierce, whipping the Pilgrim's cloak. Visual: The Pilgrim stands before the massive mound of stones left by thousands of others. He reaches into his pocket for his own stone. Audio: "The Boundary Rider" (Acoustic Guitar).

Lyrical Integration: As he holds the stone—representing his past burdens—the lyrics sync with his movements: "I've been riding the fences of the heart's high ground, Looking for the places where the wire's come down."

Action: The Pilgrim looks at the stone. He remembers a moment of conflict from his book—a moment where he felt "fenced in" by his own ego. Dialogue (V.O.): "We build fences to keep the world out, but we only succeed in locking ourselves in." Action: He drops the stone. Audio: > "Leave the gate open, let the spirit run wide,

There's no more need for the rider to hide."

Scene 7: The Cafe and the Ghost

Location: A small, stone-walled cafe in the Cebreiro fog. Visual: The Pilgrim is writing in his diary. The door creaks open. THE WOMAN enters. She represents the "Magdalene" figure—the love and the longing from his past books. Audio: "Oh! My God."

Dialogue:

- The Woman: "You're still writing, I see."
- Pilgrim: "I'm trying to find the ending."
- The Woman: "There is no ending on the Camino. There is only the 'now.' You told me that once, in a garden a lifetime ago." Action: She smiles—a sad, beautiful smile—and leaves a shell on his table. She exits into the

mist. Music: The lyrics of "Oh! My God" highlight the divinity found in human connection and loss.

The silence between them is heavy with years of unspoken words. Audio: "Oh! My God" (Piano-led, soulful).

Lyrical Integration: The song acts as a bridge between his memories of her in the "familiar garden" and her presence as a fellow pilgrim.

Dialogue:

- Pilgrim: "I see the garden every time I close my eyes. I see you there."
- The Woman: "The garden was a classroom, but the road is the exam."
- Audio:

"Oh! My God, I see You in the morning light, in the face of the stranger, in the middle of the night. In the love I lost and the grace I found, On this dusty, holy, ancient ground."

Action: As the lyric "Oh My God" plays, she places her hand over his on the wooden table. They embrace, and she cries out, as if in lovemaking, "Oh MY God." It is a moment of total "Discernment"—recognising the divine in the human. She stands to leave, and he realises he no longer needs to chase the memory; the memory is part of the light he carries.

Scene 8: The Finale – Santiago

Location: The entrance to the city of Santiago de Compostela. Visual: A montage of "Quiet Music." We see quick, beautiful shots: a hand reaching out to help a fallen walker; an older woman handing an orange to a pilgrim; the rain falling on the Galician green. Audio: "Santiago" begins its crescendo. Action: The Pilgrim walks through the narrow streets. The sound of his staff on the cobblestones echoes. He passes under the Arch of the Palace, where the bagpipes usually play, but today, his song "Santiago" fills the space.

Lyrical Integration: As he walks the final meters toward the Cathedral, the lyrics provide the ultimate resolution to the "Quest" started in Scene 1. Audio: "Santiago, you've been calling my name, through the wind and the shadows and the burning flame. The road has ended, but the walk has begun, Beneath the golden light of the setting sun."

Action: He looks up at the statue of Saint James. He isn't crying from exhaustion, but from a profound sense of arrival —not at a building, but at a state of being.

Final Shot: The Pilgrim stands in the centre of the Praza do Obradoiro. He looks up at the Cathedral. He is no longer the "Santiago Traveller" searching for something; he is the man who has found himself.

Fade to Black.

Soundtrack Cue Sheet: The Santiago Traveller

Scene / Location	Track Title	Timing & Emotional Context

I. The Pyrenees / Orisson	"The Quest"	Intro: Starts with a wide shot of the peaks. V.O. Sync: The About Us speech enters at 0:45 as he reaches the summit. The music drops to a whisper for the Song of Roland verse.
II. The Roncesvalles Woods	"Walking the Camino"	Beat: Rhythmic and steady. Plays as he meets the younger pilgrims and the Spanish Girl. It represents the "Physical Camino"—the joy of the legs and the road.
III. The Chapel Transition	"Lead Kindly Light"	Beat: Contemplative. Begins as he kneels in Roncesvalles or Leon. It is the bridge between his physical exhaustion and his spiritual "Discernment."
IV. The Familiar Garden	"Magdalene"	Beat: Soft, melancholic, nostalgic. Fades in during the "Memory Dive" scenes. It symbolises the love he is discerning—moving from the pain of loss to the peace of memory.
V. The Meseta / Hornillos	"Love"	Beat: Acoustic and intimate. Plays as he reads the note from the Spanish Girl: "Thank you for being my companion... I kiss you." Here is the "Grace" beat of the film.

V I . Meeting Brother John	"Santiago Traveller"	Beat: Powerful, grounding. Starts when the "David-like" monk appears. The lyrics reflect the Pilgrim's internal struggle to keep pace with a man of such immense spirit.
V I I . Foncebad ón Ascent	" T h e Boundary Rider"	Beat: Reflective. Plays as he climbs the final hills before Galicia. It signifies the "Fences" coming down —the ego being left at the Iron Cross.
VIII. The Arrival (Santiago)	"Santiago "	Finale: Full arrangement. Begins as the pilgrim sees the spires from Monte del Gozo and reaches its peak as he enters the Praza do

Final Script Polish: The Closing Image before the location at Finisterre

Location: Praza do Obradoiro, Santiago. Visual: The Pilgrim sits on the wet stones. He pulls out the Crucifix given to him by Brother John and the Note left by the Spanish Girl. He looks at one, then the other. Audio: The final chorus of "Santiago" fades into a single, sustained violin note. Action: He looks into the camera. For the first time, he isn't a "Memory Diver" looking into the past. He is a man looking at the world as it is. Text on Screen: "Based on The Camino Diaries and The Sword of Discernment." Fade to Black.

Location: Finisterre, overlooking the vast ocean at the zero marker **Sound:**

Scene `.

Wind. Distant ocean. No music yet. Just natural sound. Wide-angle 180-degree view of the coastline. Cuts to a pilgrim at the wild ocean beach at Fimisterre, retrieving a piece of driftwood. He notes its mahogany. A scene of contemplation before he discards it, then cuts to Muxia near the church on a rocky ledge overlooking the ocean.

Visual:
Wide shot. Old pilgrims stand alone on the rocky coastline at Muxía.
The ocean is vast, restless. Mist rolling in.
Voiceover (soft, reflective):
In the end…The Camino was never about the road.

Scene 2 – The Ocean Breathes
Visual:
The young pilgrim turns back to the sea.
I, an old pilgrim, turn in the opposite direction… and begin to walk away into the mist.

– Music Begins
Sound:
The opening notes of *"Teach the Children"* begin—soft, almost distant.

– Walking into the Mist

Visual:
Long shot. Old Pilgrim figure fading into the mist.
Wind lifts your clothing. The world is quiet.

Voiceover (now blending with music): Not in rejection…
But in understanding. Because the Camino does not ask us to escape the world… credits roll down the screen as the music continues.

– Final Reflections
Visual montage (slow dissolves):

- The empty road stretches into the horizon
- A pilgrim walking alone at sunrise
- A close-up of worn boots
- The ocean is calmer now

Voiceover:

It asks us to walk within it differently.
Quietly. Gently. Without the need to take more than we give.

– The Message
Visual:

The young pilgrim remains at the ocean, holding the crucifix.
Voiceover:

Not as an outward show…but as a light. For others.

– Final Wide Shot
Visual:

A vast aerial shot of coastline and ocean. Endless. Timeless.

Voiceover (final lines, spaced, breathing with music):
So the journey continues…not on the road…but in the way we live. Walk gently. Let go when the time comes.
And listen…to the quiet rhythm of the heart.
Because it is there…that the true Camino…never ends.
 – **Fade to Black**
Sound:
"Teach the Children" rises fully now.

Credits Roll

Visual: Black screen → slow fade of credits.
Music:
Full song carries through.

Optional Final Touch (Powerful Ending Image)

After credits begin rolling, one last visual fades in briefly:
A single pilgrim walking toward the horizon.

Then gone.

About the Author

Doug McPhillips, poet, singer, songwriter, and author, commenced his journey of discovery over a decade ago after life-changing experiences.

The Many tracks he has traversed throughout the Northern Hemisphere and down under in New Zealand and Australia have resulted in his writing thirty-three novels across a wide range of genres.

Doug has recorded and sings songs related to his work with majestic melody in true Australian style.

Doug is an adventurer who divides his time between creative pursuits, family and friends, and those who may benefit from his efforts and experiences.

Worldwide Publishers
IngramSparke
1 La Verge TN37086
Nashville, Tennessee.